JAMAICA BILTMORE; CASH, GUNS & FLY RODS

BY

THOMAS GRECO

Chapter One

Private Eye

The day starts as any other summer day might on the hot westside of New York City. It has been over ninety degrees for the past twenty days, and it's beginning to get old, to say the least. On a good day, the haze only hovers over the street like a mirage. On a bad day, the asphalt pavement melts faster than ice cream in a microwave.

My name is Jamaica Biltmore, and I'm a private eye. I run a restaurant bar, which also doubles as an office for me and second home to my son, Joe.

Having a semi-grown-up son adds to the hard days and long nights I encounter in this business. Like most eighteen-year-olds, Joe prides himself on usually doing just the opposite of what I would like him to do. No matter how much it hurts me, he is insisting on going to college next year, when I would like him to follow in my footsteps and work with me. I have even explained to him that few careers let you shoot people and not get in trouble for it. Sometimes.

Joe's Dad's Place is located on Tenth Avenue, between 34th and 35th streets. This is a tough neighborhood, even

1

on a good day. It doesn't help that this area of the city seems to be stuck in a time warp, from around 1946. I would have been right at home with the private eyes of that era. Jack Gettes in Chinatown is one reason I decided to become a private eye. Those times had a special feel. Everybody wore cool-looking hats and drove classic cars. All the new restaurants around town love the 'look' of our place, (as if we did this on purpose) and have tried to copy it.

The bar has not changed since I inherited it in 1978; in fact, it has not changed since my uncle bought it in 1950. The regular crowd loves the atmosphere. We even still have the tin ceiling and the original wide-planked wood floor. On the walls, there is wood paneling about five feet up, and white plaster walls from the top of the paneling to the ceiling. That right there dates us for sure.

Joe is working the long mahogany bar, serving coffee to the regular clients who come by in the morning for their caffeine fix. The regulars love to hear about the gossip from the night before. Behind the bar, the liquor bottles on their stepped glass shelves are reflected in a vast ceiling-high mirror, the kind that always gets smashed in the cowboy movies. The overhead air conditioning unit is already humming right along with the jukebox.

The place is shaped like the Big Dipper, the wood and glass entrance door being located in the handle. In the rear are ten wooden tables that make up the dining room. I'm standing at the end of the bar reading the sports section as I watch Joe out the corner of my eye kibitzing with the patrons. For a kid of eighteen, he has a wonderful personality. He can chat as comfortably with a senior citizen as with someone his age. They can't teach that in college. The lunch crowd has yet to materialize, which is a good thing since my cook called in sick again.

I'm starting to run out of time with Joe. I need one good case to convince my son that college is for the average guy, while my work has adventure written all over it. I make my own hours, and granted sometimes I don't work at all, but I do have this place to fall back on. I'm my own boss, but sure I also act as the cleaning man and the gofer. I can even pay myself what I'm worth, though sometimes I make less money than the kid selling newspapers down the block. On the other hand, the ladies think my line of work is adventurous and exciting. That's all I need.

Chapter Two

The Client

The heavy door opens, and the piercing morning sun seems to go right through the figure standing in the doorway. I should take this as an omen, but I don't believe in that mystic stuff (this would have been a good time to start, I later realize). The heat of the day follows the man in. His body has as much starch as his white shirt.

I get many suits in here, but this one looks oddly out of place. Thomas Degan speaks as well as he is dressed, I notice. For someone who could be no older than me, forty-five, he looks years older. A triple bypass is written all over his face. He approaches the bar very tentatively, looking around as if somebody is following him. I've seen this look before.

I leave the corner of the bar to see if I can help him. My instincts say this guy is in trouble; I put my paper behind the bar (disgusted with the Yankees blowing another late lead) and head his way.

"I'm looking for a Mr. Biltmore. Mr. Jamaica Biltmore," says the suit to no one in particular.

Joe looks up from the cup of coffee he is pouring for himself and points to me.

Sometimes he slips back into being an ordinary eighteen-year-old kid, especially when someone comes in looking for me. He doesn't have much confidence in the case of a lifetime walking into our lives, neither now nor anytime soon. One of these days, it will happen.

"I'm Jamaica Biltmore. How can I help you?"

The suit looks around. "Is there any place we can talk?" he inquires.

I motion him to the end of the bar, but he looks troubled as he heads my way.

"Is this as private as it gets?" I look around the empty place and at the two people at the bar plus my son.

"That's my partner, and these people don't even know you are here. What can I do for you, Mister…?"

Thomas Degan goes on to explain that he owns a large construction company here in Manhattan. He and his partner have been quite successful in bidding on city contracts for road construction lately. They are the new kids on the block though. They both have construction in their family, although he never explains what he means by that. He and his partner have invested in a lot of equipment recently, and there have been subtle threats against them over the last couple of months. Nothing concrete though. They thought it was just the competition getting scared of the new kid. That is the good news, I presume.

But now it seems his partner, Robert Martelli, has disappeared. That must be the bad news. People always start with the good news and then follow up with the bad news. I guess they think it will lessen the impact of the bad news.

Of course, I ask the usual stupid questions regarding his partner's girlfriend, disgruntled workers, possible debtors, you know— the type of dumb questions you hear on all the bad television shows. Unfortunately, they are the only questions that come to mind. He gives me all the vital information regarding his partner, and as I am about to mention my fee, he hands| me an envelope stuffed with cash. I like this guy already. Finally, a down payment.

He glares over his shoulder as if expecting someone' still very nervous. "This is a matter of life and death. I don't think this will end with Robert."

He starts to make his exit, when he stops and flings a business card onto the bar, and only then proceeds to the door. I am now standing behind the bar. He turns and stares at me.

"There'll be others looking for him. This is not your usual missing person. This business of mine can get rough when people poke around," he says sternly.

My response is to produce a pair of nickel-plated 9mm handguns that I have stored under the bar. "I'm a cautious type of guy," I reply. (Damn, I always wanted to do that!).

Mr. Degan opens the door and disappears into the bright sun. The look on my son's face is priceless, one of pure disbelief. I can't help but crack the faintest of grins.

"Dad, this macho gun stuff has to stop. It's silly. This is a missing person case. I got ten bucks that says this guy has walked off with his secretary. Nobody is killed over this anymore. There'll be no shooting people today, Dad."

I replace my handguns under the counter and stroll over to the large window in front of the bar. I want to check out the car that brought Mr. Degan. Degan is already pulling away from the curb in a black BMW convertible, the top-up. Nice car. The car one drives says a lot about a person. I drive a 1968 Corvette.

Time seems to tick by, frame after slow frame, like an old nickel movie. As Thomas Degan gets to the corner, a construction flagman working at the end of the block waves him to stop. A large dump truck backs up around the corner. The truck's backup warning beeper does not seem to be working, which I find a little strange. The flagman is still holding up traffic. Degan turns around just as a dark sedan pulls right up to his rear bumper, making backing up also impossible.

Both Degan and I look back towards the dump truck at the same time. All at once, I leap back to the bar and grab a gun, shouting to no one in particular to call 911. The flagman is gone. The driver from the sedan leaps from his car and disappears from sight as I bolt through the front door. Degan seems to be paralyzed. Why isn't he getting out of the car? The dump truck, now right up over Degan's car, lifts his bed and dumps fifty tons of asphalt onto Degan, neatly pinning, then burying him in the car.

By the time I reach the car, it's too late. Hot steam rises from the mound of asphalt that used to be his car. Within minutes, my son joins me at the scene of the dumping. The hot streets have become hotter. Traffic is building up to ten cars deep back to our place.

"Another great client, Dad," Joe says, looking on with amazement. I can see by the look on his face that he does not like the smell of hot asphalt. I love that smell.

I look at him with excitement in my eyes, "We have not heard the end of this guy." As I finish, I see the lights of the police cars stuck in traffic at the end of the block. There is no way we can make it back to the bar before the police arrive.

Within minutes, the streets are crawling with cops. A crime scene is set up faster than a three-card Monty game in front of Macy's at holiday time. One young cop is directing traffic around the now burning hot asphalt-filled car. From behind, I hear a voice that always gives me comfort.

"Once I heard the address of the 911 call, I figured you'd be involved," Captain Caruso says as he puts his hand on Joe's shoulder. "Doesn't college look better and better each day?" Not waiting for an answer, Caruso looks at me and then at the car. "Another friend?"

"I swear I had nothing to do with this," is the best I can think of.

Captain Tom Caruso has been a friend since school days on Long Island. We left high school together, only to join the Navy on the same morning, much to the distress of our parents. We both got lucky and did not see much action except for getting in trouble in as many southern ports as possible.

After our tour of duty was over, we stayed close. He joined the police department, and I worked as an insurance investigator and slowly made my way into this great world of being a P.I. Insurance companies no longer had guys like me on the payroll. They felt it would be better to have us as independent contractors. I think it had something to do with their image and ours.

Caruso has saved my ass numerous times with the higher-ups in the police department. He also knows I am kind of a cult hero with the young cops who look for a more exciting life than writing parking tickets and directing traffic at crime scenes.

Most of the cops here on 34th street know me quite well. They have all watched Joe grow up during the hard times after his mother left us. I have done the best I can, which most would admit is quite well. We have done more things together in his short eighteen years than most parents do with their kids in their whole lifetime.

I have taken Joe all over the world in search of the perfect fishing spots. In those years, he has learned about the world and become a well-rounded kid. All this time together has left a great mark on him as well as me (including the time in Spain when we got involved in a missing contessa case and were almost tried for treason. He was twelve and thought it was very exciting. He wrote about his summer in a Spanish jail when he went back to school in September. I had to explain to his teachers that he was never in any danger.)

Caruso suggests we head back to the bar to talk. I figure I have about fifty feet before I reach the bar to come up with a semi-good story to take the heat off both of us. Caruso will have to answer his bosses about my involvement in this morning's little incident. He needs something to take back to the station house to keep his butt out of the fire. Even a captain has to take heat for a crazy friend.

After all, it was my idea to join the Navy after a futile night of trying to pick up girls at an old crusty Long Island bar named Tabered Ale House.

The idea was to arrive early at the bar so we could at least catch the first wave of girls that came in early. Unfortunately, the night was uneventful as usual. Soon, it was three in the morning, and we had struck out again. Life in Wantagh was boring as hell for us, or so we thought.

The next morning, we fulfilled our beer oath from the night before. When we arrived at the Bethpage recruiting station, completely hung over, the staff sergeant was thrilled to take us. Nobody in their right mind was signing up for the navy in 1972, since the draft was still in effect. The recruitment officer even bought us breakfast. He was going to make his quota for the month.

Nobody said we were in the right mind, especially our mothers. This was still a big dilemma for our dads. They fought and saved the world from the big bad Nazis, and being patriotic was as important as apple pie and the '65 Chevy Impalas we all owned. However, Vietnam created a big internal problem as the so-called "war" raged on.

As we broke the news to our parents, I could see the rage in their eyes, not to mention the stupidity they saw in ours. They even questioned how they raised us.

We were going to join the Navy and see the world. Ha! The four years we spent in Key West and Norfolk, Virginia was like an endless spring break with nice clothes that drove the girls crazy.

After being discharged in 1977, life was not much better at home, except we were starting to grow up. Caruso passed the test for the New York City police department, and I got married. A relative got me a job working as an insurance claims investigator, which was as exciting as watching the traffic on the Long Island Expressway on the Fourth of July.

After Joe was born, I got laid off, and my darling wife left us both for a trip around the world with a cruise ship captain. Reports from Bali eventually had her stranded without any money or a passport. And after a dead body showed up in the restroom of the bar I had inherited from a stupid dead uncle, I decided to branch out on my own. The thrill of solving the case was like nothing I had ever felt before. Caruso, who was then a Lieutenant, got me a gun permit, which validated my life as a private eye.

Now, fifteen years later, Joe wants to break his father's heart by going to college instead of following in my footsteps. Some kids have no regard for their parent's feelings. However, this just might be the case to bring him over to the dark side.

We have a bet. If he shows the slightest interest in my work, he stays home and goes to night school, and works with me part-time. (Unfortunately no gun for part-time work) If he shows no interest at all, he gets to go away to the school of his choice. I intend to make this a great case.

Caruso said he would even help turn over a couple of dead bodies to make this case fun. That's what friends are for.

Chapter Three

The Explanation

We arrive back at the bar. Joe goes around the end to pour the iced coffee for Caruso and me. Caruso motions me to a stool next to his with a little pat on the wooden seat.

"Jump up here little boy, and tell your Uncle what the hell this one is about."

I have trouble containing my laughter. Then I have a brainstorm. I will tell him the truth. I never have tried that so soon into a case. Joe would be impressed. Moreover, I did not have anything to hide - yet.

I went straight for the truth about this guy coming in and asking for help in finding his missing partner, Robert Martelli, and all about the construction business and the subtle threats they have been receiving or think they have been receiving.

Joe almost falls over the bar, spilling the iced coffee. Over the years, Joe has gotten used to my outlandish tales. Now I have pulled a straight one. Caruso asks if the guy gave me anything like a check or a business card. I think Joe is going to burst when I do not mention the envelope with the cash, but let's face it, cash is cash.

Caruso looks at me sternly from his stool and stares. "Stop telling such outlandish tales, and stop turning minnows into whales." At least that is what I imagined he has said. That is Dr. Seuss creeping into my brain again.

My explanation is shorter than the time it takes Caruso to put one sugar into his iced coffee.

"You will call, right?" Caruso asks, just as he gulps down his iced coffee. He gets up to go and heads for the door.

"You'll pick me up, tonight? Right?" I refer to our planned outing to Yankee Stadium.

"Of course, we would not want you taking that car of yours out at night," Caruso says sarcastically, walking out the door without turning around.

Phillip Meli, a good friend, fellow fishing nut, and world-famous writer is staring at me from his end of the world. Phillip holds court every day from early morning to sometimes into the night, from a worn-out bar stool at one end of the bar, depending on who needs his service. Most of the time I do.

Phillip and I met while I was in the insurance business. He knew every scheme possible in fraud claims. He was a natural crook, who also happens to be a great mystery writer when he feels like it. I was introduced to him when I was working on a stolen car ring and my case took me to Jamaica. Caruso, who was becoming a rising star in the police department, gave me Phillip's name as a possible lead, or at least a person who might know something of value in the case.

The connections that Phillip had throughout the Caribbean were incredible. The police never trusted Phillip though, and he was always a suspect in anything that had a connection with the lower latitudes.

The fact of the matter was that Phillip had family ties on some of the islands and had fished at all the remote ports since he was a kid. He made enough money on some early books he had written to allow him the time and money to do as he pleased now.

This lack of occupation led the police to keep a close eye on him until Caruso finally came on one of our many fishing trips and realized the police were being led on a wild goose chase by a mystery writer whose fish stories were part of his life. Phillip loved the ruse.

Yes, the car case in Jamaica was also how I became known as Jamaica Biltmore. That is a story for another time.

Phillip, Joe, and I do not know what to make of the day's events. Even I must admit that this day is something new. Hopefully, it's new enough to keep Joe wondering what will happen next. Even I was curious, mostly about what hot asphalt does to a human body, but curious nevertheless.

The rest of the afternoon is spent listening to Phillip drone on about the construction industry.

The mob and the construction industry apparently first came together when unions started their stranglehold on American cities. The unions had something the mob loved, money by the boatload. Union dues poured in month after month. The mob decided the best way to get their share was by being in the construction industry itself, so they controlled certain trades, like concrete, drywall, plumbing, and so on. Now, they had money coming from all ends of the industry.

Building developers and owners were all interested in one thing, labor peace. The last thing they needed was their new building never being built, or worse. their existing building being shut down because the owners did not cooperate with the mob. Payoffs were a small price to pay to keep their businesses going. Combine this with the mob's control of the docks and the trucking industry, and you had tight control over the entire city. Even city officials cooperated at times, knowing that if they did not, one phone call could shut down the entire city (the garbage strike and union unrest in the '70s was still fresh in people's minds.)

This education would come in handy.

. There is a hint of curiosity in Joe's voice as he asks Philip many questions. I think this case has struck a chord with him. How could it not, with a mysterious client who winds up dead from hot asphalt, and a mysterious, gorgeous lady watching us from afar? I think I was the only one who noticed her in a red Mercedes, watching with more than morbid curiosity from across the street as we went back to the bar. Sometimes things just strike me as not being right.

Chapter Four

Who's On First?

Caruso shows up right on time. We never miss batting practice. One of the perks of being a Captain in the police department is using a cruiser when your car is down for repairs. Tonight we'd need it. Traffic is backed up over the Tri-Borough Bridge.

"Put your sirens on," I say as I reach over to flip the switch. Caruso slaps my hand.

"What's the use in having a badge and not using it?" Caruso is not listening to me at all. I'm giving directions to avoid the traffic, and he's listening to the police radio.

We make our way slowly over the bridge; Caruso gives a short blast of his siren.

"Now you're showing your stuff." Up ahead I can now see the cause of the traffic. Six cop cars with their lights flashing have closed off two of the three lanes. Since this is Caruso's night off and not his territory, he will only stop for a second to wave his badge around. I guess six cop cars around one empty car has gotten his curiosity piqued; either that or he's just being nosy. I know I couldn't care less; it is a Yankee night, and I feel good.

16

A cop directing traffic on the bridge makes his way over to our car. Caruso shows his badge, but the cop barely gives Caruso a second look. Cops are not impressed with other cops.

"What's up?"

"Looks like a jumper, Capt'n."

I figured it's time to chime in, or we'll be here all night. I hate missing batting practice. We have these passes from a couple of the players that allow us field access during the batting practice. The passes are tied to a very famous pitcher (who will remain nameless), who was becoming paranoid from a crazy stalker. The death threats were coming every day for three weeks, and the guy was so nervous he could not throw one inning without hitting an opposing player in the head. While he was on the mound, he would hear popping noises from the stands, and he assumed he was being shot at.

Finally, I was called in, and within a day, we had a suspect in custody. Everyone was impressed, including the owner of the Yankees who gave me a very nice autographed picture of himself. The grateful players pulled some strings and got me these passes. The pitcher went on to win the Cy Young award that year. The old lady who was arrested for stalking never bothered him again, after he agreed to have one dinner with her, accompanied by me for protection.

"Thanks, sergeant. We'll be going now."

Caruso pays no attention to me. "Divers find a body yet?"

The cop looks around, "Nothing yet."

"We'll be going now," I interrupt. Caruso looks at me and realizes he's not needed here.

"Thanks, Sarge. If we don't get to the game before batting practice, Mr. Biltmore goes crazy."

The sergeant sticks his head in the car. "Is that Jamaica Biltmore? Nice to meet you, sir."

As the words are leaving his lips, Caruso steps on the gas and pulls around the traffic. "Get that smirk off your face. A real freaking celebrity." I chuckle to myself.

We drive the rest of the way in without mentioning another "Biltmore" sighting, as I like to call them. Finally, the silence is broken by the police radio that is on low volume considering Caruso is off duty. A police radio at times can sound like a cab stuck in a tunnel with an AM station on. We exchange a quick glance as we hear…" the car belongs to a Robert Martelli of Westchester, we have a note secured."

Caruso looks at me. "Two people dead in less than twelve hours, and you know both of them. The mayor is going to get suspicious."

"Let's look at this logically," I protest. Caruso laughs that smart-ass laugh.

"Let's say Degan is having a little trouble with some people….."

Caruso interrupts," Having trouble? Getting killed by ten tons of asphalt is a lot of trouble."

"It all depends on how you look at it. Why would Martelli kill himself? That's no way to protect yourself from bad guys. He could always turn to you guys for help. I shoot a deadpan look at Caruso. All right, he could always go to someone for help."

Caruso shakes his head, "Let's just go to the game and enjoy ourselves. I think you lost a great client, and his missing partner, and probably Joe too. Face it, college is not so bad. He'll come out with a real job, not like ours. I don't see either of us retiring to the Bahamas soon."

Caruso has put a damper on the whole night. The Yankees do not help our mood, as they blow three late-inning leads and lose to Baltimore.

CHAPTER FIVE

TWO ALL BEEF PATTIES

Caruso drops me in front of my place, and my gloom turns into pure curiosity. The red Mercedes is parked out front, and this time it is not hiding from us. I enter the bar to a nice mid-week crowd.

Bobby Matthew, the bartender, is keeping up a conversation with a woman who looks a little out of place here. The Mercedes owner, I presume.

Bobby has been with us since he blew out his knee during a pre-season football game with the Giants two years ago. A six-foot, three inches, two-hundred-forty-pound lost soul with a big heart, who has no other goal in life but football – that's Bobby.

He points in my direction before I have a chance to wave him off. Joe, who has been in the back of the place supervising the dinner crowd, notices the lady too and makes his way over to the bar, a chip-off the old block. My competition skills go into high gear, and I manage to arrive first, introducing myself. I barely get my hand out for a greeting when the lady interrupts.

"I'm Jennifer Degan."

<u>Oh shit, the grieving widow</u>. Panic starts to set in when I realize that she does not look like the typical widow. If she were, why would she be here? Her husband is not even cold yet. Instead of going into an apology mode, I decide to let her play out her story. I have a feeling I will not be wrong — it's a gift, kinda like playing shortstop.

"This is going to be strange for me…"

I just nod as Bobby gets me a cup of coffee. We are standing at the end of the bar when I then notice two very large looking blocks of concrete come barreling through the door. This is going to be trouble. (It's amazing how quickly I can see things happening.) The clients in the narrow part of the bar are knocked aside by my new rude customers.

I pat myself at the back of my waist, suddenly realizing my guns are now locked in my safe in the back room — not too smart. Both Bobby and Joe sense trouble. Bobby jumps over the bar and is flattened with a right cross before his feet touch the ground. (Great linebackers do not necessarily make good fighters..)

Joe rushes to help but is brushed aside by Thing One. Before Thing Two can grab Jennifer by the sleeve, I hit him hard with the base of my palm, right in the nose. This shot is generally either very effective or very stupid. This time it works, and blood flows like a broken water main. When done correctly, this open palm punch to the underside of the nose feels like a swing of the bat from Reggie Jackson trying to hit a fastball out of the park. Your eyes fill up with water instantly.

Thing Two reacts, throwing me up against the dartboard. I grab a handful of darts and throw them as quickly as possible at Thing Two, missing of course. I grab the dartboard next and hit Thing Two in the face. Whoa, that hurts me more than him.

The crowd is behind me, not a very comforting thought. Thing One and Thing Two, feeling outnumbered though, and losing lots of blood, stumble out of the bar. Jennifer, who has witnessed the whole episode from the side of the bar, seems relieved.

"Drinks for everyone," bellows Joe quickly.

I help Bobby up and take him to the office in the rear of the bar next to the small kitchen. Joe follows with an ice pack. Looking over my shoulder, I see Jennifer following us. She has some explaining to do.

Bobby sits at my desk as I hold an ice pack to his head. Joe, sensing I'm about to lose my cool, goes back to the crowd to restore order. I notice that Jennifer watches Joe very carefully.

"Let me explain," She looks at me for a response, which I do not offer.

She continues. (I feel like Humphrey Bogart right now. Usually, I feel like Maxwell Smart, so this feels good.)

"I was coming here to hire you as my husband did. I need you to find Robert Martelli as quickly as possible. His life is in danger more now than ever." (I always find that expression very stupid— redundant, to say the least.)

I cannot believe my ears. Her husband was just turned into a human highway and she is thinking about her husband's partner. Just as bad thoughts are streaming through my brain Joe returns. Jennifer looks at Joe with some sort of weird sympathy.

"He's my partner, Joe this is…" She inserts, "Jennifer Degan."

Joe starts in," I'm sorry about your husband." I am about to cancel out his condolences when I realize that I'd like to see how she handles this. As expected, she kind of dances around it and continues her story.

"Look, Mr. Biltmore, I've been in love with Robert Martelli for years and my husband knew it. We were married in name only. I know it wasn't right but too many people were involved and would not allow a divorce to happen. It's very complicated."

Now, what do I do with the information regarding the possible suicide of Mr. Martelli? Bobby grabs the ice pack and walks out of the office.

"Thanks for the help, Bob. Why don't you take the night off? Your head has got to be killing you."

"Not as much as yours will be." Bobby walks out.

How this night is going, I figure I'd spill the beans about Mr. Martelli. I tell her to sit down as I re-tell my story of the evening including the bridge episode. By the time I'm done, Joe's eyes are bulging and Jennifer's are dripping.

My curiosity is now piqued. Why a grieving widow would be chased by two thugs is something she'll have to explain. Obviously, somebody wants to keep her quiet. Boy is that a Private Eye 101 reasoning! This case is looking like a Twilight Zone episode where everyone involved ends up dead in a very strange way. Wait a minute, this case has no paying client. At least no live paying client. The cash did come in handy. I hate when that happens. Either I need her to hire me right this minute or I cut my losses.

"Mr. Baltimore, I need you to find out who is behind these killings. My husband was leaving me and I wanted to spend the rest of my life with Mr. Martelli. I knew Thomas came to see you from his appointment book. Their business was growing and Thomas was being threatened when he tried to expand it. They were after some big-city construction contracts and I heard a couple of names that kept coming up from Thomas and Robert, a Myron Cohen, and Al Burns. They both work for the city. I know Thomas did not trust them."

Joe has a puzzled look on his face. I see I'll need to teach him how to hide his feelings. Poker face. I was confused as hell but I hid my expression.

"You look confused Mr. Biltmore. Don't worry, it will clear itself up," Jennifer gets up to leave.

"Where can I find you?" I ask. She hands me a card and I put it into my pocket.

"My associate will take you home." I motion to Phillip with a steering wheel sign. He puts down his coffee and walks over.

No one can trail him. He has a keen understanding of underworld thugs. He knows how these guys operate. Mob guys all act the same, just like all cops and accountants act the same. Phillip will know right away if anyone is trailing him. They all buy their cars and clothes from the same place. On the first day of mob class, they learn how to follow someone. Use a dark sedan and have two thugs the size of New Jersey in the front seat wearing black shirts and dark sport coats.

Jennifer sticks out her hand. I gladly take it. She turns and follows Phillip out of the bar.

"Why didn't she just go to the police to find out who killed her husband and boyfriend?" Joe questioned.

"First, my good boy, we must try to hide our expression. Granted her story was a little strange but she is a paying customer and the story was something that not even Phillip could make up. There is something else cooking here. She's hiding something from the cops."

As we walk from the back of the bar, my mind starts drifting to the lesson from Phillip earlier in the day. The construction industry and the mob are a lot different from a stray husband or a simple kidnapping case. This is dangerous stuff. The jokes about cement shoes have a lot of merits. Wherever there is a lot of money to be made the mob gets involved. They love violence. That is their only strong point.

The rest of the night goes by uneventfully. Phillip comes back, gives us some warning about the group of people we are dealing with then asks if he can come along to help if things get rough. I can always use another tough guy.

Bobby suggests he come a long too, for protection. I glanced at my merry band of men and figured that from this point on I'll carry both guns. I now have a handful of people to protect. I go home to get rest. Tomorrow will be big. To city hall, we go— me and my merry band of misfit P.I's.

CHAPTER SIX

YOU CAN'T FIGHT CITY HALL

I walk to the bar around ten a.m. and find Joe, Bobby, and Phillip planning the day. They decide to take two cars to city hall, a lead car and a trailer, just in case we are followed. We will use one car to divert our follower's attention. Yeah right, I think to myself. A diversion my ass. I'll lay ten-to-one that we separate in three blocks.

I decide to go along with the plan. Joe seems excited. I ask Bobby if he still has his football helmet. He does not get the joke. We depart into the sunlight. It's the gunfight at the OK Corral meets the Marx Brothers. The plan is Joe will ride with me in my mint condition 1968 Corvette. I hate using this car for work. Bobby and Phillip will follow in Bobby's Jeep Wrangler. And to think they have been planning this part since seven-thirty. What the hell, they're having fun. They're bubbling over with private eye stuff. Good. That can't hurt.

We get into our respective cars and I start pulling out. I explain to Joe that he should follow my lead when we get there. I don't want to spook these two fellows. I reach up and adjust the rear view mirror so I can get a better view of things behind us.

Bobby and Philip are already three cars behind and we've just left the curb. They seem to be in a very animated conversation. This scares me to no end.

Traffic to city hall sucks. On the way, I instruct Joe as to what we can and cannot say. My cell phone rings and Bobby wants to know where we are. I explain how to get to city hall and where we will park. I don't think it's helped much. He needs to get out of the bar more. We finally pull into a Meyers Parking Lot about a block from One Centre Street. I give the guy an extra ten dollars to park the car in a good spot. We wait around ten minutes to see where he puts the car. I want to make sure my ten goes to a worthy cause. Bobby and Phillip finally pull in. The attendant takes their car and pulls in rather fast right next to mine. If he gets it any closer it could be in my trunk. The four of us head across Broadway towards our destination.

Joe and I make our way into the cavernous old marbled lobby. I want Bobby and Phillip to lag behind. The grumpy old guard at the information desk points to the elevator bank at the rear of the building.

Joe and I ride in silence as Bobby and Philip take another elevator. I hope to God they know where they're going. I picture them riding up and down the large building looking for us as Joe and I get into trouble.

The elevator door opens to a drab, dark green reception area. A perky young girl is an official greeter to the building department. Joe takes the lead, which surprises the hell out of me. Nevertheless, the girl is cute.

"Could you tell us if Mr. Cohen is in?" Joe says with a cute look of his own. This is sick.

The girl explains, as if we care, that this is her first day and she has no idea who Mr. Cohen is but will check with somebody. The girl turns to ask a worker who walks by her desk. He seems to be in his own world and takes a good long minute to answer her. He looks annoyed and just points down the hall. Our receptionist shrugs her shoulders and gives us a pass to enter behind her. Joe sticks around to make small talk but catches up with me as I'm reading the nameplates next to each door.

At the next-to-last door I see the nameplate I'm looking for — Mr. Cohen. Next to the last office —must be important. Well, as important as a city official could be. I walk past this door to see who occupies the last office. Mr. Burns, Chief Building Inspector. I look in. I see two desks filled with two large, mean pit bulls – secretaries to Mr. Burns.

Joe walks past the secretaries to Mr. Cohen's office and knocks on the door, but does not wait for a reply and barges in. Not a good thing. What the hell, I did that to Cardinal Keating at St. Patrick's Cathedral once but that's another story.

"Can I help you?" Cohen snaps, half rising out of his seat and slamming down his phone.

I quickly glance around the room, as I like to do to get a feel for a person. I see many photos of buildings, builders, and big-time people including my two dead clients. The same old gray-haired man seems to be the common denominator in all the pictures.

Myron Cohen is a wormy-looking man, middle fifties, slightly bald, about one hundred and twenty pounds soaking wet with weights in his pockets. Obviously, he's a front. Wormy-looking guys are never the leader. I figure it's time to take over.

"Were looking for information regarding City Wide Developers."

Cohen gives us the once-over from top to bottom. He tries to be casual and not draw attention to the fact that he has hit a button under his desk.

"You two do not look like the owners of that company," Cohen concludes.

I inform him that we were hired to look into their complaints that were filed with the city regarding Winterfield Developer. Just as Cohen finishes his statement, the doorway fills with two substantial gorillas. Bad guys always seem to travel in pairs; it raises their IQ. One looks a little more polished than the other, but gorillas nevertheless.

"Maybe I can be of help. I'm Al Burns, Commissioner of Building Inspection." Al Burns looks around sixty. The white hair gives him an air of legitimacy, but to me, he's a thug in drag.

"I'm Jamaica Biltmore and this is my assistant, Joe. And you are?" I nod towards the silent, beefy fellow hiding behind Al Burns.

"He's with me," Al gives us. Al motions for the big guy to leave. Strong, stupid, and silent — the perfect employee.

"Please come in and let's talk about this", says Al as he walks across the room to stand behind Myron Cohen who is still chewing his lunch. No class.

"Very impressive wall," I say to Myron to get a reaction. Nothing.

"We're very busy here. City Wide Developers got angry because they lost out to Winterfield Developers on a few projects. The projects were quite large and they needed the jobs to put them on the map. It's that simple, fellas. This is a tough business. I think the hanky panky going on between husbands and wives has something to do with it if you know what I mean. I don't understand airing dirty family laundry in public. I know my son would never take our problems outside the home," states Al Burns.

You can see the anvil falling off the cliff as if Wil E. Coyote was aiming it right at my head. My face lights up like a neon sign. Al reads it like a beginner-reading book.

"Let me guess: nobody informed you that Thurston Winterfield and Thomas Degan are father and stepson? Oh boy. Look, guys. You've wasted more of our time than we can afford. Stay out of this for your own good," He strides out of the room as his final words echo in my head.

Myron has a smirk on his face that I will hopefully wipe off one day.

Sensing we are done, I pull at Joe's sleeve. I notice Al and the ape talking at the end of the long, drab, green corridor. They are deep in conversation and the ape is wiping something black off his hands. In his pocket is a large wrench. Al Burns sees us and walks toward us, alone. We meet at the elevator lobby. Al gets there first and presses the button for the elevator, acting very cordial. The elevator arrives and he holds the door for us. Joe and I get into the elevator—alone.

Just as I hit the lobby button in the old Westinghouse elevator, I put it all together. The black on the ape's hands was grease, and the wrench was used to do something to this elevator car. Oh shit. Joe looks at my face and senses something is wrong. This is good. We're starting to be on the same wavelength. It took Caruso and me a long time to be able to do that. I guess being blood has something to do with it. I just hope we get out of this to do it again. I jump up and hit the ceiling hatch that leads out of the elevator and onto its roof. Without hesitation, I boost Joe up through the hatch. He turns and pulls me up. The elevator does not make the fast descent like in the movies because the emergency air brakes are catching hold of the cables.

From the roof of the falling elevator, we are able to jump to the adjacent elevator. In most elevator shafts the elevators are only two feet apart. It's not Indiana Jones, but I'll be achy tomorrow. We lower ourselves through the other hatch and I immediately hit the first-floor button, much to the surprise of the other riders in the car. The door opens and I pull Joe towards the stairwell, racing down to the lobby.

The ape is there with the building manager, trying to open the fallen elevator, obviously hoping to find two pancaked bodies. I silently make my way over to them. I tap him on the shoulder and clock him in the jaw. Big guys fall hard. Bobby and Phillip are nowhere to be found. Some back-up. I go to grab my cell phone and pull out broken plastic and scrambled wires.

I pull Joe, still dazed by our latest exploits, away from the growing crowd. A security guard stares at us but makes no move. He looks for instruction from the manager who is leaning over the fallen goon. We exit through the antique revolving door to the large courtyard leading to Centre Street. We quickly make our way across the street through throngs of rushing people.

This area of Manhattan makes me very nervous. One Police Plaza is nearby, and the thought of this news getting to my buddy before I can explain worries me a bit. I need to get Joe back to real-time. He's still out there somewhere.

We enter the parking lot and I see ten people looking to get their cars out. Joe still has the dazed look on his face from the elevator ride.

Staring at Joe, I offer, "Let's get a bite to eat."

CHAPTER SEVEN

FAMILY AFFAIR

Making a right from the parking lot onto Broadway, we walk for a block, then enter a dimly lit bar. As we enter, the entire crowd turns as if it is the catena scene from Star Wars. From a back booth, I hear the familiar accent of an old acquaintance. The bartender-bouncer looks concerned and seems poised to make a move if we are undesirables. The elderly man at the back table peers out from the booth, sensing the bartender's reaction to the 'intruders.'

I call out to defuse the tension, "Uncle Gino, what's the good word?"

Gino Partenza rises with open arms to welcome us. We give each other a good old-fashioned Italian hug and kiss.

"Gino, this is my son, Joe. Joe this is a friend of ours, Gino."

Joe extends his hand and Gino takes it and pulls Joe in for a hug.

"Sit, sit. What brings you here?" Gino sits first. In front of him is a small plate with a few biscuits and a small cup of espresso.

Gino is dressed in his customary starched white French-cuffed shirt, a tie that matches his pocket square, and a dark, pinstripe suit. Looks can be deceiving. Gino is no lawyer waiting for the judge to come back from recess.

"We were down here on business and things kind of fell through," I offer. "I thought that since we were in the area we would come by, say hello and have my son meet you."

Gino Partenza is a smart guy in a profession that does not have many. Gino came from Calabria, one of the southern-most cities in Italy before you reach Sicily. Gino arrived here in 1937 and, like many people from Calabria, settled in East New York with his parents and six siblings. Gino got involved early with the neighborhood tough guys. The bosses who used these young hoods for a lot of dirty work saw something in Gino that the other kids did not possess— brains. He never was picked up by the police for stupid crimes, like his friends were, and always seemed able to make a buck when others could not. This impressed everybody. He was one of the very few who became a made member without the usual prerequisite of killing somebody. Money was always the chief objective of the mob. Besides being tough, if you were a good earner you were looked upon quite favorably by the bosses. He rose quickly through the ranks, always avoiding the senseless wars that broke out whenever a young Turk wanted to rid the family of its dictator. Gino stayed out of the limelight while other mob guys craved it. He never became the boss of a family, which probably saved his life. He continued to make money for himself and the bosses above him, no matter who they were. Over the years, as new blood took over families, he became less known. From then on, the money he made was for himself and his close friends. He was well known to many politicians, judges, and business tycoons in the boardrooms across the country. Bugsy Siegel might have started Las Vegas, but Gino was the cash behind it.

Gino looks at me with slanted eyes. "You wouldn't be trying to get your son here to follow in your business? A lot of friends pulled that same stuff in my business and their kids spent a lot of time with their dads too – about ten to twenty!"

The joke makes us crack up. Gino motions the bartender over and gives him a hand signal to bring additional espresso and biscuits.

"Let me offer some advice, Joseph Thomas." Joe looks at Gino in surprise. Nobody knows his full name. He never uses it. Gino notices his look. "I guess your pop never told you the story about your name. Well, I guess if you're going to follow in his footsteps you should hear the story."

"I don't know if this is the right time to go into this. He's not sure he wants to do this. He wants to do something else. He's breaking my heart. He's thinking of college of all things," I explain.

Gino laughs.

"My dad thinks this is a great profession," Joe coughs up.

The bartender arrives with the espresso and biscuits. I take a small sip. I motion for Joe to try the espresso. Joe sips and barely restrains himself from spitting out the scalding hot, super-strong coffee.

"Joe, where else can you shoot people and not get into trouble? Gino here cannot even carry a gun without getting ten FBI guys knocking down his door," I mock in good humor.

I can see the shock from the morning is wearing off. Joe is relaxing a little and he's getting curious.

"How do you know each other?" Joe asks, trying the espresso again with much better luck.

Gino takes his last sip of espresso. "It started about twenty-five years ago before you were born and before your pop was married. He was working for an insurance company. Our paths crossed a lot. We kept stealing stuff and your pop tried to find it."

I chuckle.

Gino goes on, "Soon he came to realize that this cat-and-mouse game was not working. Things were different back then. We were having harmless fun until people started winding up dead and dropped on the streets. The police got pissed, and regular people did not find us so romantic anymore. The cops got serious and no longer turned the other cheek when it came to our way of life. Then, worst of all nobody could keep their mouths shut when they were caught, and everybody went to jail. However, your dad here was a straight shooter, not with a gun though. Have you ever seen him shoot? My advice to you Joe is if things get heavy, duck and hide. There's a good chance that if you are shot it might be from your dad here. He shot me once while he was shooting at someone else."

I interrupt, "That bullet hit off a concrete wall, then bounced and barely skinned you."

Gino laughs. "Imagine shooting somebody in my business and living to talk about it. See, Joe, some of us stayed lower than the radar and we actually are retired.

We have our own pension of sorts. Some of us had a brain; most didn't but who cares about them? Your dad has been a good friend for many years. We even helped him on the famous case down in Jamaica while he was chasing those stolen cars."

Joe perks up.

"You don't know about that, eh?" Gino asked. "Back in the 1980s, your dad was working on a big insurance scam. Cars were being stolen from around the country and shipped in container ships to Jamaica for transport to other countries. Good business, lots of cash, except for the people who were not part of the business. See, Joseph, when a soldier makes money in our line of work, he must feed a percent up the ladder to his boss, who in turn must give some further up the ladder to the big boss. In return, the soldier gets protection from the cops and mostly from other soldiers from other families who try to muscle in on his business. Some of us got mad since we did not get a piece of the pie from this stolen car ring." Gino played around with the cup in front of him as if trying to determine how to tell the rest of the story. "A friend of mine who was supposed to get a slice of anything that moved from the Brooklyn docks got nothing. His boss was getting his share from another source. There was nothing my friend could do. The boss got his money, so peace was ensured. The police were getting involved only because the Chief of Police's wife's new sports car was stolen right from her driveway. Caruso even tried helping your dad. Everyone thought if your dad went down to Jamaica with the backing of the insurance company, the stolen car ring could be broken up. Your dad had some big connections in the islands. The police could not go themselves at the time because of the red tape in going to another country. Well, your dad goes down to Jamaica with a buddy of his—"

"Phillip," I interject.

"Yes, Phillip. What a character. The police suspected Phillip was — how do you say — associated with me and my friends, but he was snowballing them and having some fun to boot. I love that guy! So picture this: boats unloading stolen cars in broad daylight, hitting the docks of Jamaica, your dad and his buddy flying into the country and seeing the action from the plane, and me and my friend planting all the information possible with the police and the insurance company to stop the stolen cars and our associates from making money because we did not get our share. It was great." Gino shook his head at the memories. "What we did not know was that your dad had a friend in the customs business that put pressure on the Jamaicans to stop this activity. In broad daylight, your dad heads a raid on the docks. The ring is smashed and before you know it another ring is operating on another island, making more money than the last operation, but no more police cars are stolen and now the right people are making money."

Joe is awestruck, "Why didn't any of those fellows come after you? You did cut off their money."

I respond, "It seems the group that set this whole stolen car ring up had stopped sending money up the ladder to the bosses. These fellows are no longer a problem. So as a bonus for shutting down the stolen car ring, the good guys and the bad guys nicknamed me Jamaica."

Joe is shaking his head, "What a great story."

I look at my watch. "We better get running. We have some people to see." I get up. "Gino, it's always a pleasure."

Joe extends his hand, "Thanks for the insight. I have a better picture of things."

Gino takes his hand, "Keep an eye on him. If you two ever need a good lawyer, remember my son, top in his class and recently made partner." I knew we should have left earlier.

Chapter Eight

Cementing a Relationship

Walking down Broadway towards our car, Joe is very silent. I wonder what he is thinking. Questions will come when he is ready, it needs to sink in. He has a lot to think about.

"This is some life you lead," Joe says blankly.

I'm not sure if this is a good sign or not. I try to process if this is a plus in my war to get him to stay on with me or not. Hopefully, this does not push him into the unthinkable, going off to college in another state. I figure I will try to smooth things over while we drive to Winterfield Developer's office uptown. We make our way to the parking lot. The attendant goes for my car and is back rather quickly, screeching the tires as he pulls up to us. Bobby and Phillip have finally left the building. I see them walking toward the parking lot. Some backup. I walk around the car making sure there is no damage.

"Nice backup, guys."

"We watched from across the lobby as you clocked that guy. We stuck around to watch. It was very amusing as all these city workers came down to see what the commotion was. I overheard one of the guys calling somebody and telling him he should expect you two," Phillip explains. "Where have you been?"

"We stopped at an old friend."

"How is Uncle Gino?" Phillip asks.

"Just great. We'll meet back at the bar. Try not to get lost going back."

We pay the parking attendant and pull out of the lot onto Broadway and head towards Sixth Avenue from a side street.

Joe is very quiet. I look over. "Do you think you could get this type of life experience in college?"

Joe laughs a sly laugh. A breakthrough.

"Look, son, that stuff you heard from Gino was from the old days. Most of my cases are simple and it leaves me a lot of time to enjoy myself. There is nothing wrong with that." I look at Joe as I finish my ridiculous statement and before I can take it back.

"You call a falling elevator, a man crushed by hot asphalt, and an attack in our restaurant a simple case? That's crazy. We could have been killed."

I want to interrupt and assure him that we couldn't have been killed during the hot asphalt incident since we were not there when it happened, but I figure I'll keep my mouth shut for once and let him go on. I hear that talk is therapeutic.

"These couple of days will cure me of having a good time in college and make me work hard on my studies. If that's what you had in mind, it surely worked," Joe confesses.

I put an expression on my face as if I had just eaten a worm. Oh boy, I hope this did not backfire. Thank goodness traffic is light. We pull into a parking lot next to a three-story turn-of-the-century brick warehouse/office building on 10th Avenue. It seems the whole block is owned by Winterfield Developers. His signs are everywhere.

I take care of the attendant and Joe waits for me next to the building. The sidewalk is closed off with a couple of barricades due to a newly poured cement sidewalk.

Out of the corner of my eye, I spot a ten-ton cement truck bearing down on us. The sound of the diesel engines gives away any plan he had to sneak up on us. I push Joe out of the way, through the barricades, and into the wet cement as the truck crashes into the parking lot attendant's booth. I do a nifty shoulder roll into the street just like in the movies. The only difference is this hurts. I grab one of my guns. I make my way to the truck, not wanting the driver to get out and continue his attack. I keep an eye on Joe who slowly pulls himself from the wet cement. He looks like he is trying to free himself from a bed of gum on a hundred-degree day.

I turn my attention back to the truck and notice that the cab is empty. The parking attendant who dove out of the booth is walking around in circles, mumbling about his boss killing him for destroying the booth. I run to Joe who is trying to do his best impression of a dog coming out of the ocean and trying to get the water off his coat. This is funny and the smile is hard to hide. There is a slight smile on his face too. I pull him from his potential cement shoe factory towards the front of the office building. I have a thought, not a good one, but a thought nevertheless.

"Since we're here we should at least ask some questions. Or should I say I will ask some questions while you stay outside and harden up?" Joe gives me a look but I think he understands never missing an opportunity no matter how concrete the evidence is. I'm glad I did not say this aloud.

As we walk, his shoes squeak. Very funny.

"Of all the places to push me, into the cement!" Joe whines.

"Sorry, it was a gut reaction," I respond.

"Your only son almost gets run down by a cement truck and you don't even get the guy?" Joes asks.

"I was more concerned with your safety. You stay out of sight while I go up and talk with this guy Winterfield."

Joe looks around the deserted streets. "It's not safe out here."

I agree. "Come into the elevator lobby and wait for me."

Joe looks at me with that stare I've come to know. "I did not say ride in the elevator; you're getting paranoid. I have work to do. Don't worry about me. I can take care of myself. I'll send your college tuition check out tomorrow."

Joe backs off, "Boy, people say moms can lay on the guilt pretty good; you're not so bad yourself."

"I was pretty good, right?" I boast.

I reach into my holster and pull out one of my guns and try to hand it to Joe. "No thanks, I'd rather get run over by a cement truck than use one of these. Did you ever have to use one?"

"Now is not the time for this." Joe looks through me. "A couple of times. I'm a bad shot anyway; they just look good."

Just then Joe is startled by a fast-moving, noisy garbage truck approaching the building. We freeze as two guys run from the rear of the truck. Joe reaches for the gun in my outstretched hand. The men grab three garbage cans from the front of the building, empty them in the rear of the truck and speed off. Joe lets out a sigh of relief. He reaches for his handkerchief in his back pocket. He pulls it out to wipe his face. He doesn't see that it is loaded with cement and proceeds to wipe more wet cement onto his face. I see this coming a mile away but cannot resist watching. A laugh is always a good thing right after almost being run down by a ten-ton truck.

Chapter Nine

Bamboozled

As I get off the wood-paneled elevator, I realize I made a good decision to leave Joe in the marble entombed lobby. I can imagine the damage wet cement would do to all this expensive wood. He'll get over it. I just hope a car going by does not backfire fire or he'll try to shoot the poor fellow.

I pull a bullet clip from my pocket. I wonder if he needs this. I flip it and put it back into my pocket, "Na."

You can tell class by the d√©cor of the reception area of an office. If this is the case, then this company is full of it. The pretty young receptionist is dwarfed by the large reception desk. The granite transition top hides a flat-screen monitor and a large bank of phones. The dark paneled wall proclaims in gold letters, 'Winterfield Developers.'

"Thurston Winterfield, please," I say with an air of – 'I belong here even though you don't know me.'

Without missing a beat the receptionist smiles, "He's expecting you."

She gets up and leads me through a hidden door within the paneled wall. The door opens into a large conference room. The receptionist walks out, leaving me alone. The walls are lined with construction site pictures and other accolades of Winterfield Developers. My eye catches a picture of Winterfield and Burns. Aha! Now I know why I was expected, though I'm sure they figured I'd be a lot shorter from my elevator ride.

Through the wood and glass wall that separates the conference room from the long corridor, I see a distinguished fellow approaching. Perfectly coiffured gray hair, gold cufflinks, monogrammed shirt (just in case he forgets who he is), polished fingernails, and red suspenders – what ego. This is the same guy from the pictures in city hall. Winterfield bursts through the door. He extends his hand, showing off a gold watch as round as a half dollar and as flat as a sheet of paper.

He starts right in before I can breathe a word as to why I have come.

"My son — or should I say my wife's son — should not have raised so many problems. He knew how this business works. Did his complaining lead to his death? It had better have not or I'll be getting mad and somebody will pay. He could have been president of this company. We are one of the largest, most profitable developers in this city. My stepson and his zealous partner started making noise about bid-rigging, and there are certain companies out there who do not like to hear a noise like that if you get my point."

Winterfield walks around the large African mahogany table to one of the pictures hanging on the wall and points to the mayor of the city.

"The mayor is a personal friend of mine. This could have been Thomas's candy store if he was smart. I know you have friends on both sides of the fence too. I've checked." Winterfield turned around to face me. "Whatever she is paying you, I'll double it. I want my son's killers found. My son's wife was trouble from the beginning, as you can imagine." He clasped his hands behind his back and walked to the front of his desk. "I doubt she told you everything. She's been a thorn in the side of the family ever since my stepson married her. She saw the spotlight of this business and pushed my son and that Martelli character into trying to become me. All she had to do was stay out of the picture. Thomas took on this Martelli guy to try to grow his business. I think his wife knew this guy before Thomas brought him on as a partner. Ever since that time, things went downhill. She could not keep her greedy hands off the business or Martelli."

As Winterfield's last words drop from his mouth he thrusts his hand with the gold, wafer-thin watch at me, signaling an end to his talking and my listening. As we shake, he walks me to the door. Kind of a good-bye pull. "Think about my offer Mr. Biltmore, and for your health, stay away from Jennifer."

Like a bad magic act, I'm in the reception area and Winterfield is gone. I head for the open elevator; I check up and down the hall looking for anybody with greasy hands.

On the ride down I have an image of Joe being a gargoyle in front of the building. As I reach the lobby my fears are alleviated. He's not hard yet; just his clothes are stiff. He's walking around the lobby like Frankenstein but without the outstretched hands. Very funny.

Chapter Ten

Hard Story to Swallow

As we leave the lobby I see a swarm of police cars around the parking lot booth, or at least what is left of it. Good old Captain Caruso is walking around with that look on his face. My built-in-excuse-making mind is working overtime. I'm on computer overload and I'm about to blow a circuit. I cannot process a story fast enough, and this has me worried.

It's not that I lie a lot, but I need to fabricate a story that will appease Caruso and keep me out of jail.

Caruso looks at me sternly. "Did you plan on reporting this?"

"I was not driving the truck," is all I can muster.

Caruso throws his hands up. "Your son said it almost killed you both."

I glare over at my hardening son. "It missed us by two feet." I turn to Joe, asking, "Did you call him?"

Joe looks shocked that I would ask him, "No, he just showed up." Something is fishy.

"Are you going to tell me that a world-famous homicide detective would just show up at a small accident scene? I find that hard to believe."

"We got a phone call of a hit and run, and it was a slow day."

I nod, "Well you're right, the cement truck hit the booth and the driver jumped out and ran. As you can see, we're both alive."

I look at them both, "Look we've got to get going before Joe turns into a diving board."

Joe and I walk past Caruso who hits Joe on the back. The slap produces a loud thud. Caruso laughs.

"We'll talk later," Caruso says as he heads for his car. He barks some instructions to the uniformed police officer working the accident scene.

The attendant brings my beautifully detailed car without us even asking. I ask if he has any plastic and he looks at his crushed booth. Joe waddles to his side of the car. God, I wish I had a camera. I remember I have an old body bag in the trunk, and quickly retrieve it. It was a gag gift from Caruso. It'll cover the leather seats of the car nicely.

"I'm glad we have your car," Joe states with a stiff upper lip (literally).

I have many comebacks, but I don't think he would appreciate any of them right now. Joe is having trouble getting in the car. I'm watching in amusement as Joe bangs himself free of the dried cement, which allows him to bend his legs. He slowly gets into the front seat as if he has just had his appendix cut out. A dozen cops are having a coronary watching this procedure. I drive slowly past them and raise my eyebrows and smile. In the rearview mirror, I see a few of the cops doubled over in laughter. Joe only notices us heading uptown.

"What the heck are you doing?" Joe blurts out.

"I thought I'd head over and have a talk with Jennifer; I think she's hiding something. Thurston Winterfield seemed very concerned about his stepson but didn't like Jennifer. Something is confusing about this relationship."

Joe shakes his head in disgust, "Could we at least go home so I could change?"

I look over at him and, with a pause that would make Chevy Chase proud, I nod and make a turn, heading for home. I don't know if this is the time to bring up our little bet.

"So, are we enjoying this case?"

Joe gives a little laugh, " Let's see, a guy gets killed by hot asphalt, another jumps from a bridge, an elevator free-falls with us in it, two monsters try to kill you in the bar and a cement truck runs me down. I think I covered everything, and you ask if I'm having fun?"

"Yeah, what's your point? Could you get this type of field experience in college? There are no internships that offer this, plus you got to hold a gun; it wasn't loaded but nonetheless, it was still a gun. I hope you are giving this a real chance. Kids today can be so cruel. How you could choose to go away to college over staying home with me and having fun is beyond my thinking." I sit in silence, hoping my speech will hit home.

Joe laughs, "Boy, talk about turning on the guilt. You'd make a good mother."

"I thought I had."

Joe looks pensive. "Dad, you've been great as a mother and father. This has nothing to do with being a good parent. This stuff looks a little dangerous, that's all. However... I promise to give this a fair shake. At least Jennifer is pretty. If she looked like Aunt Joan I would've been in summer school already."

Just then the car phone rings. I pull it from the cradle. Joe sees the worried look creeping across my face as I race past the turn-off to our house.

"What's wrong dad?"

"Bobby's in a jam."

We ride in silence to the abandoned railroad yards on the west side of 46th street as instructed on the phone. I try to visualize the place in my head so I can formulate a plan before we get there. (Something new. I guess Joe's presence has had some influence on me.)

"What kind of jam?" Joe interrupts.

"Somebody kind of borrowed him for a while."

"You mean kidnapped him!" Joe blurts out.

I laugh, "Borrowed is a better word. I think that somebody is trying to kill us again."

Joe's face turns cement pale. "Why again?"

"Well you see son, when people like this miss, they take on Avis' motto, and they try harder next time."

CHAPTER ELEVEN

TRAINING WHEELS

My experience tells me that, in a situation like this, it's best to let the events dictate what type of action to take. In other words, I do not have clue what to do and I'll just wing it. We slowly make our way past the rusted-out abandoned freight cars that litter the train yard. I see a dark sedan parked next to a pile of old railroad ties. I turn off my lights, put the clutch into neutral, and turn off the ignition. We coast silently next to a boxcar to hide our approach. I cannot help but think about the damage all these rocks are doing to the underside of my car. I need to stay focused. We get out; I hand one of the guns to Joe.

"Do I get bullets this time?"

I pull a clip from my pocket just as three shots kick up dirt around our feet. Joe freezes in place. I push him behind the large, rusty, steel train wheels to protect him from the bullets. I look through the cars and see Bobby seated on the tracks with his hands tied behind his back. Next to Bobby is a pair of legs walking back and forth. I aim and hit the exposed leg on the first shot. I see Myron Cohen fall to the ground.

I exclaim excitedly, "Look who it is our friend from the building department. What a small world."

I notice another pair of feet scurrying away from the fallen Mr. Cohen. Overcome by a sense of confidence, Joe whirls around and notices the other man headed for a car in the distance. The huge ape-in-a-suit from the elevator ride turns and fires an errant shot at Joe, missing badly. Joe returns the fire rapidly, shooting wildly. I wave my arms, trying to get Joe to stop.

"This is not the movies. You're going to run out of bullets, and we have to explain each one to Caruso."

The shooter has driven his car to where the fallen Cohen is bleeding all over the tracks. Cohen gets himself up and manages to throw himself into the backseat of the car, screaming in pain. We run over, but not in time to stop them from getting away. They leave in a cloud of dust, racing down Tenth Avenue.

Joe bends over to untie Bobby just as five police cars with sirens blaring come screaming into the train yards. They slam on their brakes, sending a cloud of dust all over us. The police jump out of their cruisers with guns drawn and take cover behind their car doors.

The sergeant notices me. "Oh shit. Somebody call the captain and tell him what we have here. How many shots did you guys fire? We're going to be here all night."

I look at Joe, "Two shots, and one hit its mark, honest."

The sergeant has an incredulous look on his face (he knows me) then barks into his radio, "All clear. I'll take over from here." The sergeant notices the dark blue, late model Ford slowly pulling into the train yard.

"You know Jamaica, I'm going to give you a police radio so you can notify me when you're on a case and I can go on vacation and miss all this exciting paperwork."

Caruso pulls up slowly. Joe has not yet untied Bobby's hands. He grabs his shoulders and pulls him to his feet. They both silently look at Caruso and me. Caruso pays no attention to anybody. He grabs me under the arm and pulls me away from the listening ears. Everybody freezes, expecting me to get an ear full.

I start protesting, "I had nothing to do with this…"

Caruso cuts me off. "This will go away, and shooting up an abandoned train yard doesn't worry me. I got a call that Thurston Winterfield was taken off the street by three thugs in broad daylight right in front of the Plaza Hotel. What do we make of that?"

I roll my eyes. "What a great case! Let me ask you something: Would you leave to go to college after experiencing a case like this?" We both look over at Joe who is trying to cut the ropes from Bobby's hands with his small, red Swiss army knife.

"You would have shot the rope off him by now," Caruso gives up.

I give him a bragging smile.

Caruso continues, "You also would have shot him in the back of the leg." Caruso laughs. "For somebody who uses a gun as much as you do, how come you can't hit anything?"

I didn't have the heart to tell him that I did hit the guy this time. I figured we'd both be in more trouble with a guy walking around with one of my bullets in him.

CHAPTER TWELVE

COMING OVER TO MY SIDE

It was time to head back to the bar and chip away at Joe. We bid Caruso goodbye and I promise to get back to him within a few hours on the Winterfield disappearing act. One of the cops will give Bobby a ride back to my place. Thank goodness; I only have a two-seater. I have only one dropcloth-bodybag to protect the seat I have, and that's for Joe who is still a mess. The last thing I need is two people messing up my car. As we get into the car I cannot help but notice that Joe is getting harder. In the rearview mirror, I can see Caruso waving his arms around, motioning everybody to get out. There'll be no investigating here. I see the yellow caution tape coming down as we leave the scene. I don't want to say that Caruso is obstructing justice with the turnstile crime scene investigation, but he knows when he's wasting time.

"What do we have planned?" inquires Joe, which is very surprising, to say the least. I see a glimpse of interest in his eyes.

"Well, after we chip off your clothes, I figure I will make some phone calls to some friends to see if they have heard of Winterfield vanishing."

"You know what I think, Dad?"

This is definite interest peeking through.

"I think there's more to this guy than just a crooked construction worker." OK, it's not a true revelation, but it shows some thought.

"Go on," I prod.

"I think we need to look into his connections with the city. Everybody has a boss to answer to. Maybe he's got some skeletons too," Joe theorizes.

This is not so bad. I've been thinking along the same lines. "I have a friend who works for the Post; if Winterfield was up to something, he'll know. He knows everything about these types of characters in this town."

Jimmy Fields is a celebrity and well-known in all circles – he writes, acts, hosts a news program, and, most important, is a syndicated columnist for the *New York Post*. Most people just look at him as another celebrity TV host. What people forget is that he started in this business riding in cop cars, chasing down everything from deadbeat traffic ticket offenders to the forgotten murders in the worst part of this city that never were reported because the dead person had no one to care about. He hides his gritty writing style in his celebrity clothes.

CHAPTER THIRTEEN

BOOK OF REVELATIONS

We arrive back at the bar and slowly make our way through the crowd. Thank God for this business; without it, I'd need to find a real job, and that would suck. I don't know how people do that. I forget that Winterfield's stepdaughter is still a paying customer. Bobby is right behind us. Phillip is holding court at the end of the bar. He tries to motion me over, but I need some coffee before I bring him up to speed. Joe walks past the curious crowd right into the backroom to change.

I slide behind the bar to call Jimmy. He'll gladly come right over for a free meal. I pour myself a cup of coffee. Just as I top off my coffee cup, I see Joe coming out from the back room, still cemented over, with a lady in tow. The woman is wearing a disguise of sorts: tight jeans, a baggy sweatshirt, and a baseball hat pulled down tight. It takes me a second to recognize Jennifer Degan, my client.

She stops when she sees me at the bar. She motions me to come to my office. This covert operation of hers, along with my son, has attracted the attention of the entire bar and dining area. As I grab the coffee and head for my office, I pass Joe and Jennifer who pull a U-turn and follow.

"I have some news," Jennifer starts before we enter.

It's time for me to put on the P.I .appearance. "I've heard. Winterfield is gone, snatched off the street. Anything you've forgotten to tell me?" I ask dryly.

Jennifer is staring at Joe. I offer, "When we went to visit Winterfield this afternoon, somebody tried to make us into a slab of cement."

"This is getting out of hand," is all she says.

Just as she finishes, there's a knock on the door, just like in the movies. Jimmy Fields walks in and Jennifer's face opens up wider than a double garage door. Jimmy's hand is out quicker than a Roger Clemens's fastball.

"Hi, I'm Jimmy Fields," he states to Jennifer, hoping she'll be impressed. She is very impressed. Ready to put a stop to the foreplay, I intercede.

"What have you got?" I ask.

"What's for dinner?" is Jimmy's reply.

"Whatever you want; what information did you find out?"

Jimmy can't keep his eyes off Jennifer. Joe understands that nothing productive is happening here. He grabs a few clothes from the closet and walks out without saying anything. Jimmy finally looks at me as if to ask whether he can talk in front of Jennifer.

"Jimmy, this is Jennifer Degan. Her husband was recently killed and Winterfield is her father-in-law or something like that. It's a long story. Tell us what you've found out."

Jimmy takes the coffee from me. "Maybe you two should sit down; this is good. It seems Winterfield went to Vegas a lot."

I interrupt, "My aunt goes to Vegas a lot."

Jimmy tries to ignore my interruption. "He did not go for the shows. He was a big bettor of sporting games. Let me give you a little history of sports betting. Years ago you could go into places like Binions Horseshoe in Las Vegas and place a hundred-thousand-dollar bet and nobody would bat an eyelash. They welcomed that type of betting. These days you step outside for a smoke between bets and the next thing you know they won't take your next bet. (My eyes are starting to glaze over. Jennifer is flat-out mesmerized with Jimmy.) It seems Winterfield was a big bettor who saw an opportunity in the making. He had plenty of cash, rich friends who liked to gamble, and contact in Vegas. Lo and behold, these off-shore gambling joints started springing up throughout the Caribbean. Winterfield was the man behind this."

Jimmy takes a long hit of my coffee. My disk drive of a brain is about to go into overload trying to process all this information. This is a tough one, considering I was barely paying attention for the first part of the story. I sense a large gap between the events of the last few days and the larger picture of Winterfield skipping town.

Joe walks back into the office. "What have I missed?"

We all give him the <u>are you kidding</u> look. Where do Jennifer's dead husband and missing partner fit into this equation? This no longer seems so straightforward. Most things in this business are. I've come to realize that most people are not as smart as they think — except this Winterfield character. We need to connect the dots amongst the New York City building officials, possibly two dead construction company owners, a gambling ring stretching to the Caribbean, and one missing tycoon. Winterfield seems to be the common denominator.

Did Winterfield set up his own disappearance? Did his stepson know anything about gambling? And most of all, how do I get Jennifer to pay for my trip to locate these gambling casinos?

"Now can we have dinner?" Jimmy finally asks.

I can't let this opportunity slip by. I turn to Jennifer, take a deep breath, and ask, "What's our next step?"

Without blinking a beautiful eyelash she starts, " I still think he's behind my husband's and Robert's murder. I don't care where he is, I still want to get to the bottom of this, and I'll spend whatever it takes. Now, more than ever, I feel he had these two guys killed to hide whatever he's involved with?"

Uh, oh. My conscience is kicking in. I have to ask, "What do we do if we find him?"

"I want a piece of whatever he's up to."

Jimmy, Joe, and I do a Three Stooges double-take. Here's a gal who was married to Winterfield's stepson who got tarred and feathered, in love with her husband's partner who decided to go high diving off the Tri-Borough Bridge, and now she wants to get involved with international gamblers for a piece of the pie – you gotta love it.

It's time for dinner and a glass of red wine to figure this out. Jennifer explains she has an appointment and leaves us in the dust to contemplate our next move. She slowly takes Jimmy's hand. I never thought a handshake could look so sexy. The door slams behind her.

"Well?" is all Jimmy could muster.

"Let's get a table and kick this around. Joe, find Phillip; I think we're going to need him on this."

As we sit at an empty table in the corner of the backroom, Joe brings Phillip over and all hell breaks loose. Questions, ideas, and stupid assumptions, mainly from me, pour over the table like a passing thunderstorm.

Of all people, Joe sees the light to calm things down. "Could we look at this thing logically?"

I'm sorry but I have to laugh. It's a good idea but, with the cast of characters around this table, I don't think it will be likely. All we need is Caruso to show up to add to this mess.

Phillip looks up from his iced tea, "Help is on its way."

Caruso walks into the bar and spots us through the crowd. He walks over, grabs a chair, and waves to the bartender.

"Let me guess: Good old Jimmy here has found out about the offshore gambling that Winterfield was involved with? I snooped around and found out the police had that information in his folder. Since it has no bearing on our fine city, we did not care too much about him. Do you want to know the best part? This gambling venture of his is legal. When the mob ran Las Vegas they loved those big bettors. Sure the top ten guys won more than they lost, but the rest of the tourists who traveled to Vegas to bet on sports lost more than they won. These tourists were the guys who did not have a corner bookmaker to lay their bets with. The mob was run out of Vegas for being greedy in the late Seventies. These new casino owners, the huge entertainment companies, saw great potential in these large cash cows, but they had to answer to the SEC since they were public companies. All the things the mob did under the table could no longer be done. The empty suits who sat on the board of directors of these companies did not have the balls to handle stuff like big gamblers. They worried about their image and their stockholders. The big hotels kicked out the gamblers who were betting a million dollars a week on every sporting game possible. The suits panicked when word spread about games being fixed, and all these sports gamblers got a bad rap."

Now things are starting to make sense. In the 1970s gamblers were able to bribe schools like Boston College because these college kids loved the flow of cash. All this money was tied into Las Vegas sports betting or at least the perception of Las Vegas.

"So, if we go find Winterfield, unless he's really kidnapped, there is nothing we can do about it, right?" I ask matter of factly.

"That's the way I see it. You're chasing something that you have no business chasing. Unless this Winterfield character had his son and partner killed, you're not accomplishing anything." Caruso takes a long pull of his coffee.

Silence spreads over us like a warm blanket. Then the turning point in the case takes place and, from all people – Joe. "What if Jennifer is behind this whole thing?"

Joe gets attacked from all sides.

I wave everybody off. I can use all the help I can get with this one. "Go on."

"Maybe we need to look into her background more. That was a pretty ruthless statement she made about wanting a piece of the action from her missing father-in-law. Maybe there's something more between her and Winterfield."

Boy, you can hear the rusty wheels turning in everybody's head. The waiter brings our food and the silence at our little pow-wow is broken only by the plates being placed on the wooden table.

Finally, Phillip breaks the silence. "What if Jimmy here puts his ear to the rumor mill to see what comes up. From what we've learned so far, Winterfield is very well known in all circles. I'll check through my Caribbean contacts and see what I come up with. This might be good for a road trip."

Caruso decides to add his two cents. "Maybe you should check in with Uncle Gino. He's been involved with Las Vegas since those hotels sprang up from the sand. He might be able to steer you in the right direction."

Well, it seems we all have our jobs cut out for us. After we finish dinner, Phillip and Jimmy leave the table to start their work. Caruso sticks around with Joe and me. I work on adding up the day's receipts from the bar, and Joe cleans the tables. I think I have a long teaser bait hook dangling in front of Joe, and he's circling. That was a good conclusion he came up with at dinner. Now if it only pans out.

I have a habit of getting antsy when I want information. I want it and I want it now. However, I realize digging into something like this takes a while. Joe and I are closing up for the day and I walk to the bar to get the disk from the computer cash register to lock it in the safe when Gino Partenza walks in. Uncle Gino himself in my place; something's up.

Gino grabs me by the arm and pulls me towards my office. He motions for Caruso to follow. Two friends of Gino the size of my jukebox make themselves comfortable by the bar. I motion for Bobby to get them something. Joe is surprised when he sees Gino.

"Do you want me to leave?" Joe begs off.

Gino looks at him for a second. "No, your pop here could use your help. It seems a certain associate of ours has skipped the country. I hear he's involved in a certain case of yours and a few bodies seem to be popping up around town. That is no concern of mine, but the business he's involved in, legit business mind you, seems to be getting out of hand."

"Like offshore gambling?" I throw the thought up in the air to see how it floats.

Gino, who does not startle easily, loses his composure. "Who the hell does not know about this, for Chrissake?"

"Take it easy, Gino. As far as everyone knows, this stuff is all legal; no one is after him for this. Vegas screwed themselves and now they're losing all this big-time gambling revenue. Not smart business."

"I hear these places in the Caribbean even take in phone bets from around the world," Caruso helps out.

Joe blurts out his opinion and opens my eyes again. "It must take a lot of money to support an operation like that."

Gino smiles. "The kid catches on quick. Lots of money and the competition is strong. What's out there are three different sources of money all looking to make a killing. One, friends of mine who still have big bucks to throw around; two, private corporations with cash to spend; and three, foreign money looking for the fast buck. All this leads to Winterfield. He built some of those new casinos in Vegas and, of course, those billion-dollar buildings need plenty of cash to keep them going from month to month."

Joe nodded in understanding.

"When you deal with that type of money it opens up a new circle of friends," Gino said. "These so-called friends have money to burn and a past to hide. Through it all, Winterfield never forgot his friends here. We bankrolled him over the years and he always repaid us in spades." Gino shook his head, probably in amazement. "Even when the heat came down on him pretty heavy when many of the bosses went to jail and started ratting each other out, he kept his mouth closed. Some of us who stayed under the radar put some money away for rainy days, so to speak, and he's been our little investment banker."

The silence lasts through three sips of coffee. If this was a cartoon you would see smoke coming from everybody's head, mine included. Sometimes I get so caught up in watching everybody else that I lose my train of thought. I seem to slip in and out of consciousness with what I should be thinking of, like now. I finally hit the reset button of my brain and reboot it.

I don't know what to make of all this. Could we chase him Winterfield to wherever he might be? What will we do if we find him? From what I've read over the years, guys with this much money and power can dictate anything they want to small third-world countries. No country will send him back since he is working hand in hand with the little dictator that runs the country. These leaders have too much to lose if Winterfield pulls his money and business out of their country. I wonder if anyone else is thinking along these lines.

Caruso starts, "What has Winterfield done to warrant you going after him? Unless you can tie him to those two murders. You can't go after him just because he's on some island in the Caribbean with lots of money."

Damn; another pause. I hate when people are so logical that it stops the conversation right in its tracks.

"Wait a minute; I'm being paid to find Winterfield and track down answers to a missing person. I don't care if he's guilty or not." As long as Jennifer is willing to pay, I'm willing to look.

Finally, somebody smarter than me— Joe— adds in, "Maybe we're overthinking this thing. First, we find him, and then we'll try and put some of these pieces together."

After another stupid pause, everyone nods in agreement. Gino offers help, contacts, cash, anything to protect his interest. I'll get back to him. Gino turns to leave without as much as a handshake. I take it he's very worried.

Phillip returns from a phone call. Amongst our little gang here we have many contacts to tap in the Caribbean. We need a starting place, and no one dares to say it until Phillip blurts out, "I think we need a base of operation." There's a slight pause, then he smiles. "Key West."

Nobody wants to act overly excited. The idea hits us like a sixteen-year-old boy who's just been told his parents are going on vacation and he can stay home alone for the weekend.

Caruso hits on an idea, "I could use a vacation anyway. I'll ask some of the boys in Vice what they've heard about Winterfield's operation. But I agree: Key West seems like the best place to start."

"OK, it's agreed, Key West. Joe and I will make the arrangements. Let's plan to leave by the weekend. We'll fly into Fort Lauderdale and drive down the coast through Key Largo and so on. Phillip, you get the welcoming committee prepped for our arrival. Caruso, think we can bring our guns?"

Caruso gives me a look like <u>are you kidding</u>?

"I can bring mine, but yours is out of the question. It's not a legal thing, it's more of a safety thing –for us." Joe laughs.

Phillip laughs to himself. His wheels are already turning. I have confidence in him. Caruso, I'm not so sure about it. Bringing a cop along could ruin all the fun. He'll want to do everything by the book. However, as soon as we land on some foreign island, his badge isn't worth anything.

Caruso bids us goodnight and promises to check in tomorrow with any information he gets on gambling joints in the Caribbean. I think this could be big. As I continue to clean up, I see the wheels in Joe's mind racing. This is the most exciting case I've ever been on, and if this does not get the hair on the back of his neck standing up, nothing will.

"Do we have a plan when we get down there? Are we going to tell our client what we're up to?"

I continue cleaning. "As much fun as this seems to be, we have a very important job to do. We have a paying client, two dead bodies, one missing person, and somebody trying to stop us. Things could get dicey; you have to be up for this." I hold my breath.

"Let me get this straight: more dangerous than a client who gets tarred and feathered, a runaway cement truck, a shootout, an elevator cable cut so we fall to our death, and another almost-client throwing himself off a bridge, and finally a thug who threatens you and is then snatched from the streets? What else could happen?" Joe throws his hands in the air.

Boy, would I love to tell him, but since he is sticking around after all that, I'd hate to spoil it. Things seem to get out of hand when you leave the comforts of the USA with no policeman's badge to protect you.

"Let's get a good night's sleep and meet back here in the morning to plan out the next week or so. You get going home and I'll stay too close up tonight."

"OK." Joe turns and walks out of the place.

After cleaning off the rest of the tables I head for the office. I've got a plan. I place a call to a ticket agent I know at the airport. I explain to her my plans and how many are at my party. With airlines getting cancellations all the time, finding a flight for four is quite simple. Getting a return flight with no exact date is harder. I tell her to leave it open. I promise to pick up the tickets tomorrow and take her to lunch soon. That's an easy payback for a great favor. We're on our way. I haven't seen Key West since the Seventies. It's going to be great. I rent a four-by-four from Avis. The drive south was always just as much fun as actually being in Key West. Well, almost.

CHAPTER FOURTEEN

ROAD TRIP

Caruso was right: it's a good thing I left my guns at home. They are very picky about things like guns at the airport check-in point. We board the plane and the excitement is bubbling over, even for Caruso. We have seats across the aisle from each other. Joe and I are in Nineteen A and B and Caruso and Phillip are in C and D. We look like four guys headed to Florida to fish or, God forbid, play golf. The day they let me substitute a baseball bat for a driver is the day I take up golf.

As we taxi away from the gate I notice Caruso, Phillip and Joe are sound asleep. I'm too excited. The flight is uneventful. I pass the time eating pretzels and dreaming of this adventure.

We exit the plane and you can feel Florida in the air. My blood is boiling. Joe, who has not been here before, inquires as to how long it'll be before we hit Key West. Caruso and Phillip stop on the way to the baggage pickup and look at him.

I look at my watch: "Let's see, it's two-thirty. By the time we get our bags, a half-hour, get the car, another half-hour, get through some local traffic and I'd say about — seven o'clock tonight."

Joe's eyes bulge out, "you have got to be kidding me. They don't have planes that go all the way there?"

"The scale on a map might read one hundred and forty miles but a good time can take hours; once it took two days," I explain happily.

"What?" Joe looks stunned.

Caruso laughs, "You better explain this trip to him."

"See Joe, the fun is the drive and the stops. I hope that most of the places are still around. You like seafood, right? Well, get ready for a feast that will last for hours. Think of it as a long buffet line that reaches from Key Largo to Key West."

As we approach the baggage carousel a limo driver with a sign reading 'Biltmore Party' is standing behind the security rope. Phillip goes up to him and shakes his hand.

"I figured we should arrive in style," Philip says. "Besides, these feasts you've been planning for the last two days tend to get out of hand, so I figured it was safer to have somebody else drive instead of you."

Caruso slaps Phillip on the back. "I love this trip already," then he turns to me and asks, "Are we allowed one drink at the Chart House and a half-day flat fishing, Mr. Biltmore?"

"I was thinking a couple of days for both," I grin.

CHAPTER FIFTEEN

DEJA VU – ALMOST

The trip out of Fort Lauderdale International Airport is uneventful. During the first forty minutes, we try to bring Joe up to speed about Key West. As we approach the intersection where Route 1 and Card Sound Road meet, we shout out in unison to the driver to take the alternate route. Phillip has made this trip many times over the years, but he always flies right into Key West or avoids the whole area and goes right to the islands but he does enjoy the ride with us. Before we left he was very elusive about his reasons for doing this. I have a funny feeling we'll find out why sooner rather than later.

First stop, Alabama Jack's. The best crab shack in the world. This place always was the kick-off place. We instruct the driver to pull in. It's still mid-morning, but we go right by the bar and onto the patio in the rear and order boiled shrimp and ice cold tap beer. Forty minutes later we're on the way. Everything is perfect. Even Joe is relaxed. Card Sound Road is a highway that runs alongside Route 1 but is very lightly traveled. It comes back into Route 1 around Key Largo.

For the next three hours, we hit all the same spots we hit thirty years ago, The Caribbean Club, The Seaside Shack, The Baltimore Oyster House, and any other crab house shanties we can spot.

Joe is getting into the mood as we cruise the Overseas Highway. He is caught up in the beauty of the bridges linking all the keys. As we approach the end of the road as we know it, we all explain to Joe what Key West is all about. We barrage him with the location of the naval station, Cow Key Channel Bridge, Old Towne, Mallory's Square, and wonderful Duval Street. The memories flood our minds as we regale him with stories of the past. We decide to go straight to Mallory Square for sunset, and then it hits us like a ton of bricks from a Road Runner cartoon.

"Holy shit, what the hell is that?" I ask, pointing to something big, white, and loaded with people dressed rather poorly, walking off it, looking like they are trying too hard to have fun. A cruise ship.

Phillip almost falls over from laughter.

Caruso just points without saying anything. He turns around in amazement. "There used to be a perfectly good parking lot over there, now it's a damn souvenir shop."

"I didn't want to ruin the good times you had planned in your head. These damn cruise ships invaded here a couple of years ago and the place has never been the same. Let's go check-in," Phillip suggests.

I'm still in shock. I guess that's what happens when you have a place with an actual end of the road and you can no longer go any further. All the stuff piles up like water against the dam. Eventually, the dam springs a leak. I turn towards the limo to pay the driver, "Progress sucks."

CHAPTER SIXTEEN

FISH STORY

All right, Key West was different than we remember. Things change, mainly us. There are college kids down here looking to have some fun and get a buzz on three Bud Lights, just like we did. They are looking at us as if we're ancient, the same way we looked at the old men down here thirty years ago. The only difference was that we did not wear bad Hawaiian shirts, Gap shorts, and two-hundred-dollar Air somebody sneakers.

"What are all these people doing down here?" Caruso questions.

"Tourists," Phillip says nonchalantly. He explains that this is why he flies right to his fishing island instead of stopping over here. Show off. I still cannot get over the fact that all these ships stop here and the people swarm over this place like a thousand bees over one shot glass filled with honey. It's time to check in and go fishing. We have a limited amount of time here. Our lovely client has authorized only three days down here for Joe and me. Phillip is helping pick up the tab for the rest of the trip. His last book did rather well.

We check into the Key West Motor Lodge, off the beaten track from Duval Street but still in walking distance of the action. Caruso thought it was a good idea to have a hotel close by if we go out one night and can only walk back to our room – youthful thinking.

As we enter our double room decorated in early 1975, we let out a collective sigh, all except for Joe.

"This place sucks."

Caruso drops his bag, "It looks the same. Didn't we stay here once?"

I'm trying not to remember.

Phillip, who has stayed in the best hotels in the Caribbean, couldn't care less. He makes his way in, drops my bag on the bed, and walks past us as the three of us just stare. He takes care of the limo driver and returns. He has that smile on his face like, let's get going guys.

"We have a boat waiting for us. The flat fishing guide is very good, and he'll help with our mission. He's an ex-CIA guy; very resourceful fellow to have around," Philip says.

We're speechless. Caruso makes the first move to the room that he's sharing with Phillip, while Joe and I start unpacking.

Within ten minutes we're all outside, dressed to fish. A white van pulls up and a local gets out, greeting Phillip. Long-time friend, I presume. We pile in; the van has all the equipment, fly rods, cooler, and backpacks. Our spirits have picked up. We are starting to feel good.

It's a five-minute drive to the dock. This is a sight: Blue skies, boats, clear water, and fishing. We follow the Captain to an open twenty-six-foot skiff docked at the end of the pier.

Four guys fly-fishing on that will be fun. I realize the driver is also our guide. We untie and push off.

Caruso and Phillip are on the bow seats, rigging up their equipment. Joe and I are seated port side. Joe has a look on his face as if he wants to talk. I've seen this look before.

"What's up?"

"You enjoy this stuff, don't you? You had a life down here that you guys love to remember. That's what I want, but you don't seem to understand it," Joe confesses.

It's time for the long talk. This might be it for a while. I have a gut feeling that, with an ex-CIA guy helping, mobsters, murder and a good-looking client can only mean one thing — extreme fun.

"I had different plans when I was here many years ago. The last thing on my mind was being an investigator. What was fun were the people I was with, these very same people. Life comes in stages. When you're young, you have a whole world in front of you, and the possibilities are endless until you need to make choices. Sometimes, most times, those choices are laid out for you either by design or by circumstance. In the end, it's all the same. I was never one to give too much advice because I didn't know what was right. I'm just trying to guide you along, set some examples, and hopefully, you'll make decisions that will lead you to a life where you'll look back when you're old and say – I have no regrets."

"Do you have any regrets?"

I pause, "Earlier in life I did, especially when your mom left. At first, that was hard, but then I took stock of what I wanted, whether she was still with me or not. I had you. That was more important than anything. I envisioned this scene in my head seventeen years ago when I took you fishing for the first time. This is what matters to me Would I like to be married again? Yes, but I have everything I want, time with you...."

"Which you don't want to let go?"

"Right. I have a fun job, good friends and lots of spare time to do what I like. Before you say it, I know it might not be what you like, but while we're together I should at least try to influence you a bit."

Just as I finish, our captain throttles down to idle. We've been talking so long I missed the views.

Joe and I let the scenery wash over us. The water is dead flat but we seem to be in deeper water than I'm used to for fly-fishing down here. We have gone from clear, light green water to the darkest blue on this side of my best funeral suit. I always wanted to try for bigger fish on the fly.

Phillip walks over to the captain and gets into a deep conversation. The captain, a fifty-ish, gray-haired, bearded man, hands Phillip a set of binoculars. As Phillip is looking in the distance, he motions me up.

The Captain, Jim Ryan, introduces himself again. I shake his hand. Damn that hurt.

He points eastward, "See the sixty-five foot Viking in the distance? Winterfield's boat."

Being in this business for a long time has me believing in a guardian angel of sorts and a Saint Christopher medal that my parents used to pin on my undershirt before we flew in a plane, but this is crazy. We're here one day and we find him. I get suspicious quickly.

Caruso and Joe join us. Phillip sees my disbelief.

"I called down to Jim from the bar the night we all had dinner. He's been on this for three days already."

Jim laughs, "I wish I could say I was that good. What you guys don't seem to remember is that what Winterfield is up to is very legal. I still have some contacts in the field and they knew exactly where to find him. He's out here three days a week, entertaining clients on that floating hotel. He leaves from the Bahamas."

"From what I know about this business, I didn't think the Bahamas would let his offshore gambling houses exist. There's too much corporate money in those huge hotel casinos," Caruso chimes in.

"You're right. A cop?"

Caruso nods.

"No, he lands his plane there and has his boat on Paradise Island. He's got a full-time captain and crew and he brings lots of money into these islands. He's greasing the right palms, so there's no trouble. You guys have a plan?" Jim looks at me, followed by everybody else.

I'm up, I guess. "Let's fish and talk. Fishing gives me time to sort things out. I thought we'd have a few days looking for him while I formulated a plan."

Jim laughs, "You would have been perfect in the CIA in the Seventies. There's some good fishing a couple of miles due west, right off a reef. Let's go."

Good, this will give me time to think. Caruso and Phillip return to the bow to complete their fishing gear. Joe starts unpacking his. He's never used a fly rod before; he's great with a spinner but this is new. At least we'll have a good laugh. Now I have to process a plan.

My backpack is ringing. I fumble for the phone.

A voice on the other end starts without a hello, "How's the fishing?"

I stare around. Caruso and Phillip have seen this look on my face before. They sense something is wrong. They make their way port side. Jim continues to drive.

"Haven't started yet," I reply stupidly.

"Why don't you guys head over this way?"

I start looking around. I don't see any boat in sight except – no it can't be.

"Stop looking around. You already spotted us just like I spotted you. You're welcome to come aboard. The fishing here is great. I have a few guests that won't mind. Don't worry, nothing will happen to you and your friends. The prime minister of the Bahamas hates the sight of blood," Winterfield laughs, then the line goes dead.

"What the hell was that all about?" Phillip asks.

"It seems our prey has been watching us. Winterfield has invited us to go fishing aboard his boat."

The silence is deafening. No one has a thought worth speaking. Finally, Joe nods towards Captain Jim and raises his eyebrows. A very good possibility, I think.

Phillip beats me to the punch. "You ratted us out?"

"Me." Jim continues driving away from the yacht.

"It's not what you think. He knew you would be down here before you got here, and not from me. What do you guys want to do?" Jim stops the boat.

Everybody looks at me. I pick up the cell phone and dial. "It's me; we've made contact, or should I say he made contact with us? He wants us to come for a visit to his boat. Yes, yes we're out fishing.—I'll tell you later." I look at Winterfield's boat as if I have to make sure it's there. "He's anchored about three miles southeast of Bimini. What do you think?"

I listen to my instructions. Finally, I add, "OK," and close the phone. "Let's go fish."

Caruso asks, "Who the hell was that?"

Without letting on too much, I tell him. "William Forester, an old friend who lives down here. He gives advice, no help but advice. I figured we'd need all the help we could get."

Caruso does not let on that he knows William Forester as Rear Admiral Forester, boss man at Boca Chico Naval Station.

Bill Forester was one of the first guys we met when we first arrived here. Not long out of the Naval Academy, he was one of the brightest guys you ever wanted to meet, besides being a great shortstop on our Sunday morning softball team and an avid fisherman Bill got me hooked, no pun intended.

This is how my fishing addiction started. It all started with deep-sea fishing – this is a sport that can be done sitting down while drinking beer in the sunshine. That's as close to heaven as we're going to get.. First you need deep pockets for the charter boat, tips for the crew unless you want to be chum, and food and drink for you and the other friends you take along for the twelve-hour tour.

As the captain runs the boat out twenty miles or so, the first and only mate sets up the outriggers with line and bait. Your main job is to stay out of the way while you crane your neck to keep an eye on the disappearing land. Now the fun starts. The captain starts slowing down to look for fish. (How he does this is beyond me, since tuna and marlin cruise the ocean floor as low as the submarines we used to work on.) As we slow down, the bobbing starts. This is not unlike standing on a sidewalk in San Francisco during an earthquake. This is when you realize that one fighting chair is not going to cut it. A fighting chair is like a barber's chair but you can drink from it. Now comes the excitement— not for you, but for the fish. The mate shouts up to the captain, in Spanish; either we have something on the line or this should bring in a big tip, I was never sure. The mate would thrust the fishing pole in your hand after making sure you have a fish and not a sunken ship, and push you into the fighting chair.

This is where the fight begins. If you have never tried pulling in a tuna, it's like being snagged onto a 1972 Buick stuck in the mud on the bottom of the ocean. The tuna has no intention of making this a fun day. Most other deep fish at least jump out of the water, giving you a reason for being in the middle of the ocean.

So now you're pumping up and down, trying to reel in some line before the fish decides to dive again, faster than the stock market. Then you start over again. All the time, friends are bobbing along with the boat, trying to look excited for you but trying to avoid losing their breakfast. That's their only job at this point. After hours of fight, you come to realize that you should never have canceled that root canal. You have spent lots of money and hopefully not lost your lunch for one big tuna the size of a jet ski in a little over six hours.

The strangest part of the whole experience is that the crew gets to sell the tuna on the dock, and all you get is a strange feeling while you're showering that afternoon like you are still on that boat.

After that day, I was introduced to fly fishing in the flats. Two feet of crystal clear water, no humming of diesel engines, and a better ratio than one fish per six hours.

CHAPTER SEVENTEEN

THE WAVE

A rogue wave is not like any other type of wave. It's a wave's wave. A wave that looks like a wave but really does not act like one. And it's coming straight for us as we head towards Winterfield's yacht. I see it coming, along with some unexpected floating debris that looks like a log. If you ever hit a tree in a boat while going at a good clip, it's not unlike flying off the front of your bike going downhill, and dragging your chin across the concrete sidewalk. This is going to hurt.

"Brace yourself," is all I can muster. I turn to grab the rail and Joe at the same time. I look at our captain, who does not see our water hazard approaching. His attention is on the speedboat approaching the starboard side faster than a tornado whipping through the plains of Kansas.

Who the hell wears ski masks on the water? See, when I'm out on the water, my senses go flat. Caruso sees them too and immediately grabs from his fly-fishing bag both his gun and mine. What a guy. He tosses me a gun and we both open fire at the same time.

Joe hits the deck and Phillip watches with slight amusement. He loves this stuff. Our fearless captain continues our approach toward the oncoming torpedo. Chicken on the water. Here's the lineup: our little fishing boat versus a thirty-two-foot Donzi – in other words, a Saturn versus. a Lamborghini, not good odds.

The thing I hate about shooting at someone is they usually return fire. All this action is bringing us closer to our gracious host-to-be – Winterfield.

Everything starts unraveling like a thread off an old sweater. From the aft deck of Winterfield's yacht, I see a deckhand with a long black tube in his hand, a shoulder missile. What a great thing to have on a boat. It surely beats gaffing a fish. Out of the corner of my eye, I see the speedboat gaining ground, and I glance back quickly to see the deckhand aiming his bazooka. The problem I see is that we are in line with his shot while Caruso is still loading and shooting. He notices me spinning back and forth from the shooting speedboat to the aiming deckhand.

"Everyone down!" I grab Joe and push him down.

Caruso and Phillip hit the deck, but our fearless, stupid captain is not budging. He cuts the engines. I peer over the outboard as the trail of smoke whizzes overhead towards the speedboat.

Now, the difference between a movie and this situation is that, in our case, the missile misses its target completely. The speedboat is still on course to hit us in about thirty seconds. Caruso motions to me that he's out of ammo. I make a mental note to bring up his lack of shooting skills if we get out of this.

From his center console, the captain pulls out a semi-automatic pistol and unloads it at the speedboat's engine. A burst of shots and a direct hit into the gas tank create an explosion that should have occurred with the missile. Our two masked gunmen and their speedboat are engulfed in a ball of fire. Bits of the charred boat float harmlessly toward us. We all rise slowly and stare at our hero as he turns the boat toward Winterfield's waiting yacht.

I watch as some huge body of a man grabs the missile launcher from the inept deckhand and throws it overboard.

Caruso, Phillip, and I are surveying the situation. Joe has not gotten to his feet yet.

I see that we are safe for now, so I figure it's a good time to assess the situation with all my investigative powers.

"What kind of shooting was that?"

Caruso looks at me. "When was the last time I had a chance to shoot at an oncoming speed boat from a floating bottle top in New York City?"

We ride in silence as we turn against our own wake. I reflect that we got out of this situation in good shape. Joe is finally on his feet. This is his first time seeing the damage of our handiwork. I hope he's taking this all in. I haven't had this much fun in twenty years. I have a suspicion that this little fishing trip is about to get better. We're getting closer to the Viking; I see Winterfield staring at us from the cockpit. There's a nicely dressed bunch on the aft deck. I look at the four of us, or should I say five of us if I include our secret agent captain sharpshooter?

The captain deftly maneuvers our boat right up to the yacht's swim platform. A mate is waiting for us and throws a line for us to tie up. One by one we make our way onto the floating Four Seasons Hotel. I have admired these boats from the concrete floor of many indoor boat shows. This is a two-million-dollar <u>fishing boat</u>. I could never think of pulling in a marlin while it dies a bloody death all over this waxed teak deck.

Our welcoming party consists of Winterfield, the Prime Minister of the Bahamas, a couple of nice-looking ladies, and three great big gorillas acting as bodyguards.

Winterfield makes his way to me with an outstretched hand and a drink in the other. Now he's acting like the party director on a cruise ship.

"Great to have you here. Ever been down this way before?" Winterfield gives me a backslap that almost sends me off the boat. Winterfield calls out to someone below deck to take a drink order. Winterfield starts the introductions but stops short when he realizes he does not know a single person except me.

I introduce Phillip, Caruso, and Joe as Winterfield introduces Mr. Lacey, Prime Minister of the Bahamas. We're all shaking hands over and under each other like a bad Marx Brother's routine. As we finish the greetings my attention is captured by the gorgeous lady coming up from the salon.

The lady takes our drink order as we follow Winterfield down into the salon. As he opens the sliding door, the air conditioning is so cold hits us like a foul ball in the nose. I let our hosts go in first so I can better survey the situation. When I notice the deckhand removing our fishing gear from our boat, I decide to return to the swim platform and retrieve my backpack, which happens to hold my gun.

The deckhand throws me my bag and I follow Joe into the salon and close the door behind me. Everyone is seated on the large leather settee. The salon is fitted out in teak and leather. The teak is so shiny I can see myself from across the cabin.

CHAPTER EIGHTEEN

HOOK, LINE, AND SINKER

I can't take this anymore. I don't care about Mr. Lacey and his little country. "Can we get to why we're here?"

Winterfield is leaning against a rather large teak table. The lady returns with our drinks on a tray. I think she's staring at me. I better clear my head and concentrate. Winterfield takes a drink. I see through the tinted windows that our fishing boat has been untied and is floating. I try to kick Caruso and roll my eyebrows up for him to look out the window. He glances out the window and notices our taxi just floating to nowhere. As if on cue, Winterfield's cell phone rings. He answers the phone.

He's doing all the listening. I can see distress creeping across his face. He closes the phone and looks at me.

"It seems that you have some friends who are very interested in your safety. I think if you follow me we can come to an understanding. I then can get on with my life and you can do whatever you and your merry band do."

Winterfield walks over to the door leading to a separate dining area. He opens the door and waits for me to follow. Everyone gets up. "Just him," Winterfield commands.

Quickly I must decide who would do better with the gun I'm hiding in my pack. I hand it to Caruso. Sometimes when friends know each other for a long time they can communicate without talking. "Hold onto this for me."

Obviously, this is not one of those times. "Hold your own pack," Caruso says. I raise my eyebrows and Phillip kicks Caruso in the leg. Now he gets it. Sometimes the sledgehammer to the head –or the leg— aids in communication.

Caruso takes the pack. Feeling the weight of my gun in the bag and seeing my eye movement he realizes something he should have is in the bag. I cannot believe everyone, including the waitress, does not scream out for Caruso to take my bag.

I follow Winterfield into the dining room next to the salon area. He sits at a large teak inlaid table. I take a seat on one side and Winterfield sits at the head of the table.

"That's very impressive, having an admiral in the United States Navy calling on your behalf. I had not taken you so seriously. I figured you were just some retired cop with a few good connections. Like I said in New York, this is a very complicated business arrangement. I have impressive friends who eat admirals for lunch. Let's make a deal: I'll help you solve the death of my stepson and his partner if you agree to stay out of my business down here. I know what you are thinking. Let me assure you that they are unrelated, at least they better be."

I raised my eyebrows but didn't say anything.

" I have powerful friends too, and I've checked: so far there is no connection. I'm sure my ex-daughter-in-law will pay you a flat fee if you find that Martelli character too." He shook his head in disbelief. "She's a piece of work. What do you say, Mr. Biltmore?"

I hate when people call me that. I can't put this mess together yet, but I figured it would be best to agree so we can get off the boat and do some digging on our own. Before I can say anything, the damn cell phone rings again. Winterfield grunts as he reaches into his pants for the phone.

"Yes? — He's fine. Right, whatever he wants. Call me later."

Winterfield does not wait for the party on the other end to finish. He stares at me with a silly smirk.

"From one end of the spectrum to the other end of the world, Mr. Biltmore. Now I'm really impressed. First an admiral in the United States Navy and now the head of an organized crime family. Can I be expecting any other surprises, Mr. Biltmore?"

"If my mother calls, tell her I promise to call her soon."

We both rise at the same time. I shake his hand. Taking advantage of my guardian angels and knowing our little boat has floated away, I ask, "You'll arrange for transport back to Key West?"

Winterfield chuckles. "You have a good set of eyes. Of course." He squeezes my hand in a two-hand grip before letting go. "Please don't mention to anyone that you have seen Mr. Lacey here. It's a sensitive issue."

"Not a word." I turn and walk back into the salon. I feel like James Bond. All I need is a white tuxedo jacket and a gorgeous lady. I'm on top of the world. Through the salon doors, I see our little fishing boat has drifted back towards the Viking with the help of the current or some other mysterious force.

Our hostess is feeding another drink to Phillip, who looks very relaxed. Captain Jim is pacing the floor. Caruso sees the smirk on my face.

"You look pretty cocky. Since you came out in one piece, I take it that you got lucky again?"

I am about to start bragging about friends in high places when the good captain reaches for a gun tucked into the waistband of his shorts and runs for the back of the boat. While I was gloating, we failed to see a forty-two-foot Tiara pull alongside the Viking and pick up Winterfield and his party. The captain fires off a couple of rounds at the passing boat but doesn't hit it. He shoots like me. I guess the CIA does not teach this stuff.

Sensing no danger, Phillip starts walking back through the salon toward the cockpit, "I'll handle this. I should be able to drive this baby."

A collective "Oh Shit" brings Phillip back to the rear. From the bow of the Tiara, we see the same deckhand who missed before reloading another shoulder missile launcher. That boat is a floating arsenal. Taking no chances this time, I grab Joe and our hostess and bailout port side. Caruso and Phillip follow in our wake. As we frantically swim toward our bobbing fishing boat, I look over my shoulder and see Captain Jim heaving as many life vests as possible overboard toward us. He jumps into the water right before a trail of smoke and a missile hit the Viking.

We are now fifty yards from the quickly sinking Viking. The floating life jackets are only a few strokes away.

I retrieve them and pass them around. The Viking sinks faster than a rock. The quick-thinking captain has caught up to us.

Caruso now has a smirk on his face. "You thought you had him beat didn't you Mr. Bond?"

"Talk about big brass ones! Winterfield just hung up with an admiral in the U.S. Navy and a mobster from New York warning him that we are not to be harmed, and he's got the guts to try to blow us up. You have to admire a guy like that."

"Who are you guys?" the hostess finally chimes in.

We have reached the fishing boat. Joe hoists himself in and lends a hand to the rest of us. The captain goes to the center console and reaches for his binoculars to search the horizon for our not so gracious host.

"I suggest we head back to Key West as soon as possible," Caruso offers. The captain has decided this anyway; he starts the engines and heads west.

"I guess fishing is out for the day?" I come up with.

This comment brings stares from everyone. The lovely hostess, who we now have dragged into our little mess, looks very good wet. She peppers us with more questions. "That's a dangerous crowd you guys hang out with. Why are you here?"

Finally, I give up, "It goes all the way back to New York, missing people, gangsters, Las Vegas and dead people — in other words, a fishing trip gone bad."

"FBI?" comes from Captain Jim.

Our new friend gives him a sheepish smile. "Very good, Mr. Ryan."

Captain Jim beams a cocky smile, "thank you."

Phillip, Joe, Caruso, and yours truly just stare at each other and then at Miss FBI at the same time. The words have been sucked out of our bodies collectively. One by one we all take a seat around the fishing boat. The captain guns the engine and turns to our new team member.

"That's the first time today that they all shut up. Thank you." We now ride in silence toward our destination. I figure we have about an hour ride as long as the Tiara does not show up. The G-Lady sits next to me.

"I'm Julie Waters, and you are?"

"Jamaica Biltmore." It's storytime and I'm picking through my minefield to come up with a good book.

CHAPTER NINETEEN

STORY TIME

I know we have some trouble when Captain Jim slows the boat down to an idle, walks back to the gunwale, and picks up a leaking gas line hose. It has been cut. What else is new?

Captain Jim walks back to his center console, opens the compartment under the steering wheel, and blindly feels around for his handheld VHF radio.

According to my calculations, we have been traveling about thirty minutes, which means we need to either swim about ten miles or drift at two knots an hour to reach Key West. A knot is a nautical term, much like a mile an hour, just more expensive.

"What's up Captn?"

"It seems our good friends cut our gas line before setting us adrift."

This conversation brings the cast and crew to the back of the boat. Joe looks worried. The captain tries his radio and reaches the coast guard rather quickly. They'll be right out, in an hour or two since we are in no danger. That's what they think.

Phillip handles this best. He breaks out his rod and reel and starts some lazy roll casting at nothing in particular. Caruso shrugs and joins him at the bow. The captain joins them upfront.

It's time to put these pieces together with Joe and Julie. Any conversation will keep Joe's mind off what could happen as we bob around like a cork in the middle of the ocean.

"What do you think, Dad?"

"We're fine. Our good friend Winterfield thinks we're dead. I hope."

I turn to Julie. "So, Miss Waters, what's your story?"

"Why don't you explain your side first? I'd love to hear about your cast of characters. You all look so interesting."

From the bow, Caruso adds his comments, "This should be good. Hope she can take it."

Julie looks at Caruso's back. Phillip is laughing to himself.

"Don't pay attention to them. OK, let's go. I'm a private investigator from New York City. Joe here is my son, helping out for the summer. The funny-looking tall guy is Captain Caruso from the NYPD, on vacation here in lovely Key West. The other character is Phillip Meli, a well-known author, and troublemaker. He's here to lend some humor to our expedition. The good captain is Phillip's friend, I think."

So far, she hadn't even blinked. "We're here on a missing person case. I dragged all these guys along since we have not been to Key West since our Navy days." I figured this was enough to offer up. I wanted to see what her story was.

"What has Winterfield done to get the FBI working undercover on that yacht?" My question has stopped the casting of fishing lines from the bow. We're all waiting to see if Julie will give us a straight answer.

"I guess saving my life deserves an explanation. We've been on him for a year. We're trying to track down a complicated money-laundering scheme that involves organized crime figures, politicians, and large corporations. All roads lead to Winterfield. I've been working on his boat for three months, but this is the first time he's been on it. Most of the time the Captain and crew drive around picking up Winterfield's associates and take them between the Bahamas and other remote islands. The trips are mainly recreational. Fishing, partying, and gambling. We've witnessed some passing of money but not the amount that we expected."

The guys were holding their rods, but definitely not paying attention to what was going on in the water. As Julie continued, you could practically see them sway toward us. "We started with about three billion dollars," she said, "supposedly leaving the United States about five months ago and being transferred into numerous offshore accounts, all tied to Winterfield. Our computer experts seem to have lost track of the money about three months ago. It kind of disappeared off the face of the earth. Some very powerful people are very nervous. Somebody is using the FBI as its private investigating service, I think."

Figuring this out is too easy. Winterfield has taken off with all the money. Now all his partners are after him. This is a sure way to end up swimming with the fish.

Julie continues, "I know what you're thinking, Winterfield has stiffed his partners and stolen the money. We ran that theory over a couple of dozen times too. It was too simple, and everything we have seen regarding Mr. Winterfield says he's not that type of guy. You do not get to be in the position he's in without being able to cook up some very intricate schemes. He's living large, using all this money from the investors as his personal piggy bank. Since his return on investment was so great, the investors did not mind his extremely high fees for setting up these casinos. It's a case of simple business: big-time investors do not care how much money they get charged as long as they can make more than the normal return on their investment. We think there is something else brewing here. Espionage is not out of the question. He's mixing some very interesting people-concoctions. He's drawn powerful people from all walks of life into this gambling venture, including entire countries. Winterfield is too smart to think he can get away with this."

It's time to recap. I think we're missing a big piece of the puzzle, or a lot of pieces. This puzzle is one of those thousand-piece puzzles for sure. It starts with one guy looking for a missing partner. He then becomes roadkill. The grieving widow shows up looking for the missing partner too, for another reason. This missing partner, we find out, jumps off a bridge. Next, Joe and I are almost flattened out by two henchmen who happen to work in the city planning offices. Winterfield now enters the picture. Again somebody tries to cement our relationship and Joe becomes a building block. Then we get shot at by the city goons. Then Winterfield disappears only to resurface down here. Along the way, we find the mob involved, the FBI, and God knows who else.

We've been drifting about for some time, and in the distance, I hear the sound of an engine. The captain has picked up the sound too. He reaches for his binoculars to search for the oncoming Coast Guard boat. Everyone on our little boat seems frozen in time. All heads are turning in different directions, looking for the rescuers from Key West. The land is on the horizon about a mile away. The tide is bringing us to shore; what luck.

There's something funny about the sound of an engine on the water: You can never tell exactly where it is coming from. The captain has noticed too, though he seems to be looking in a different direction.

Julie beats us to the punch: "Jet skis, at least two."

Caruso points in two directions. "You're partially right, two from the west and two from the east."

Joe looks right at me, "These odds are not so great. Any ideas?"

The captain is fumbling around his console looking for I-don't-know-what, but I hope it's good. We're down to one gun and very few bullets. The captain finally finds his missing item, a flare gun. Not bad; not good, but not bad. Caruso looks up.

"Wait for it." He turns quicker than a bobblehead doll. Then he points to the distance. The four jet skis are closing in fast as is the Apache helicopter. The jet skis don't notice the helicopter, which will make for a very interesting collision. There's nothing we can do except watch.

The captain is staring with force at the helicopter. His eyes have not left the helicopter since Caruso pointed it out.

I would love to think everything is in slow motion like the movies, but it's not. Things could not be going any faster. Everyone is yelling at once.

The captain screams, "In the water now."

Joe and Julie both spot the familiar orange and white Coast Guard cutter speeding toward us. It seems to be leaping over the water, gaining on the jet skis. The helicopter is a hundred yards off our bow. The captain aims at the helicopter with the flair gun.

Joe notices him, "What the hell is he...."

I don't give him a chance to finish. I push him and Julie into the water. Phillip dives off the bow. Caruso too notices the helicopter is not a Navy helicopter and takes careful aim knowing he is running out of bullets.

From the Coast Guard Cutter, an anti-aircraft missile is shot from the deck towards the helicopter. The captain and Caruso fire at the same time. The missile hits its mark, causing a tremendous explosion. The bullets and the flair are caught up in the explosion. I'm sure Captain Jim and Caruso will each go to bed tonight thinking they single-handedly shot down an Apache Helicopter with one shot. That's a good dream.

The Coast Guard Cutter has overtaken two of the masked Jet Ski drivers. The other two, seeing the commotion, turn on a dime and high tail it back to where ever they came from.

Joe and Julie clamber back into the boat. Phillip needs a hand.

The Coast Guard cutter eases her way to us. An officer from the bow uses a bullhorn to address us.

They will pull alongside and throw us a towline. First, of course, he wants to make sure who we are.

"Is Jamaica Biltmore aboard?" the officer questions.

Feeling like a rock star, I raise my hand.

"We have orders to keep you aboard your little vessel. We will send a tender over to pick up the rest of your party. Sorry, Mr. Biltmore. Those are specific orders from the Navy."

A collective chuckle rises from our little battle-weary group.

"You were feeling pretty big just then?" Caruso laughs.

Trying to hide my deflating ego, I say, "I'm just glad we were found."

The tender slowly arrives. One by one my crew piles into the tender. Joe is the second to last one-off. "Want me to stay, Dad?"

"Thanks, Joe, take the ride. Those cutters are pretty cool."

Joe goes over the side and into the tender. The first mate waits for Julie.

"I'll stay," she responds.

The first mate unties the tender and motors off to the cutter, which has swung around to the bow of our boat. The tender grabs the tow line from the cutter and brings it back towards where I'm standing. I use the gaffe and snag the line and tie the towline onto both front cleats.

I'm trying to hold in my excitement about riding with Julie alone. The cutter's engines are causing our little boat to bob up and down like a wine cork in a pool after a fat kid has jumped in. I have to hold onto the rail very tightly as the cutter moves a safe distance from us. Julie carefully walks to the bow of the boat. Holding on for dear life, she almost goes head-over-heels over the rail but grabs onto me for support. Very exciting.

We both finally sit on the bow cushions as the cutter picks up speed, pulling us along for the ride. It's time to find out exactly what the FBI knows.

"What's your next move?"

"I figured I'd head back to headquarters and see what we've heard about Winterfield's location. We've had a whole team of agents on him ever since he arrived from New York. Someone seems very interested in him. We never spend this much time on a case like this."

"Well, it seems he has attracted a lot of attention from all sorts of people. Politicians, city officials, old mobsters, and of course the FBI..." I think I spilled more than I wanted to. Good-looking girls have that effect on me.

Since I opened up I am hoping that she will spill more too. If that doesn't work then maybe, just maybe, when we get on land I'll hear from her again and I'll have a pipeline into the FBI. Not a bad thought.

The quick trip back to Key West passes in silence, but not in lack of thoughts, both legal and illegal. Over on the cutter, my partners are nowhere in sight. I have to admit, this is exciting. As we slowly pull into the Navy base, the cutter cuts its engines and a smaller boat comes into the bay to bring us the rest of the way to the dock.

I help by untying the pull line from the cleats and taking a new line from the arriving boat. The cutter maneuvers its way to a larger dock. We are headed for the smaller dock where a reception committee is waiting. I have a funny feeling they're waiting mainly for me. Through the crowd of people, I see William Forester pacing on the dock. The little plebes are trying to stay out of his way and out of his line of fire.

William Forester can be a pit bull at best. It took Caruso and me a long time to get on his good side. We kept ending up in his doghouse while we were stationed here, but finally, luck shone down on us one day. Caruso and I were fishing on our day off, and Forester's daughter and her boyfriend, whom the admiral hated, were spending some quality time on his little skiff when they hit something in the water.

Luckily Caruso and I jumped into the water and pulled them into our boat. The daughter's boyfriend hit his head and we saved his life, much to the chagrin of the admiral. The boyfriend did not have a job, except playing in a rock band; of course, this does not sit well with an Admiral in the United States Navy. We never told the admiral that the skiff hit a log the size of a 1972 Buick. The daughter and the boyfriend were not paying attention if you get my drift. From that point on, we could do no wrong; well, we did, but he never seemed to mind.

The admiral's daughter eventually married the guy and he went on to become one of the biggest rock stars of our time. With all his money, he bought his new father-in-law a forty-five-foot fishing yacht and a new home.

I'm standing on the bow waiting for the barrage to start. Hopefully, he takes it easy since we are in the company of an FBI agent and I would love to continue to work on this case with her. From two docks over I see my gang of four being picked up in a Navy jeep and heading our way.

The dock is a good three feet lower than the pier, which makes Forester look even more intimidating. Julie walks in close to me. Even this seasoned FBI agent looks nervous.

"That's a lot of brass on one person."

"He's a pussy cat. He has a loud bark. When he starts ranting and raving, one of the plebes here will probably land in the water." Julie laughs.

Forester lends a hand to Julie as she climbs up the ladder to the pier. Now it's my turn. As I start my climb, his big hand is stretched out to help me too. Something's up.

"Everything OK?" Forester asks as he gives me a last pull onto the pier.

"We're fine. I think Joe is a little shaken. He's been through a lot."

"Let's head back to the mess; I'm sure you've had a hard day."

There isn't a person on the pier who does not wonder what Forester is up to. This response isn't what everyone has come to expect from him. The waves stopped crashing against the dock and the seagulls stopped flapping their wings when he asked that question so politely. Everyone is stunned, to say the least. The faces of the people on the dock probably look like the faces of the King and Queen of Spain when they heard that Columbus was back. Thank God Caruso and the boys have arrived. Forester makes his way to Caruso and gives him a warm handshake. Then he hugs Joe.

"You OK?" He offers Joe.

"Just fine, Uncle Bill. I'm getting used to this."

Forester offers up, "Let's get away from the dock. We have a lot of talking and catching up to do. I'm sure Special Agent Waters has a lot to talk about too." Forester does not even get to see the surprise look on her face. He's already in the car waiting. He rolls down the window for one last greeting.

"Sorry Phillip, how are you? I could use another book when you decide to stop hanging around with these delinquents and start writing again."

Phillip chuckles as Forester rolls up his window. Phillip turns to me, "What's up with him, anger management classes finally working?"

One of the petty officers chimes in, "Not on your life. It's a shame he's retiring in a week."

That was a bombshell for me. I thought he never would leave. This is going to be one hell of a cup of coffee. We all climb into our waiting cars for the short ride to the mess hall. Captain Jim seems too quiet for my liking. The admiral did not even acknowledge him. Julie is still looking dazed. No one in her field office will believe the crew we've assembled here in lovely Key West, all being welcomed by one of the highest-ranking naval officers in the country. Talk about friends in all the right places.

CHAPTER TWENTY

CUP OF JOE

I have forgotten how small this base is. We arrive at the low pea-green metal prefab mess hall. I see by my watch that the admiral planned this visit well. There will not be a soul here. We're right between meals, not that this food is considered a meal, but I have heard that this place is Morton's Steak House compared to the others.

Caruso, Joe, Phillip, Jim, and Julie are just standing about, not knowing what to expect. I head for the coffee station with the admiral. I motion for the others to follow. I'm sure everybody's mind is racing in different directions. Caruso is thinking about how much trouble he's getting in, which could jeopardize his retirement in three months. Phillip will probably start writing again, Jim is thinking CIA stuff, Joe is scared stiff and Julie thinks I'm cute. At least that is what I imagine is running through everyone's head. I think it is time to break the ice. "What's this retirement talk?"

Forester finishes pouring his coffee, still black with no sugar or creamer; Starbucks would love a guy like this.

He nods for us to follow him. When we all have our coffee, we head to a dark corner of the room.

Caruso leans over, "He's scaring me. I thought I knew him better."

Since I know him best, it's up to me to find out what's going on. It's almost like somebody is controlling him. Nah…

As we find a bench, Forester takes a deep breath that signals a long dissertation. I was afraid of this.

"This is like the mission impossible team: cop, FBI, CIA, writer, godson, and you. Some suits from Washington came down last week to visit us. It seems that your friend Winterfield had some very important people looking for him. The FBI was watching him in New York and, when you clowns got involved, I got the phone call. If I wanted to retire as planned I would have to keep an eye on you and make sure you did not get in the way. When you called, I should have warned you to stay away. I did not think you'd catch up to him this quickly. Obviously, you had help."

I was dying to ask, "I thought you had your eye on a position at the Pentagon or the White House if the right person lived there?"

"I did. I interviewed a couple of times for Chief of Staff but something kept pulling me back here. In my mind, I would weigh that life and this one. You need to be a special person to work in Washington. My life here is full. I teach at the academy on an as-needed basis, I'm finishing my book on naval history, Rose and I travel with my daughter and that son-in-law of mine to his concerts, and, of course, there is this place. Granted it's not 1972, but it's still better than most places, and the fishing is great. I take my son-in-law and his band fishing all the time. Take away the long hair and earrings and you have a nice bunch of guys."

"Who happens to be worth fifty million dollars or so," I interject.

"First impressions are very deceiving. You know these guys give more money to charities in the cities they play than any Palm Beach rich guy I know?"

"I'm confused. I know I'm only a young kid, but something is missing here," Joe looks over at Forester.

"That's what has me so worried too," Forester laments.

Caruso stands up and starts pacing. He's got his police thinking cap on. I get up for more coffee. "Please, get started. I'll pick up when I get back."

Caruso starts. "This case has two levels. On one level we have the murder of Winterfield's stepson and the son's missing partner, which is all tied into the construction business in New York, which of course would explain the mob connection. Then, on a higher level, we have Winterfield and some big money people involved with an offshore gambling operation and the mob getting nervous about their missing money. We have the FBI looking for that missing money, though we are not sure whose money, besides the mob's, is missing. If it were only the mob's money, why would the FBI care? I think we have more money invested with Winterfield than meets the eye. I have a gut feeling we have political money invested in these gambling paradises too."

Joe interrupts, "Every time we get near Winterfield, somebody tries to kill us. If they were after him, why not just kill him and forget about us?"

Walking back to the table the anvil lands on my head. As I process Caruso's thoughts, I come across the missing link. This is why I'm so good. You have to be able to link people together who have no business being linked. This is why criminals get away with their crimes for a while until people like me put it all together.

Phillip sees the smile on my face. "Oh boy. Sherlock Holmes has something."

A hush falls over the crowd.

It's time to go in for the kill. "What if Martelli is not really missing; maybe he did not kill himself? Maybe, just maybe, he and Jennifer have been plotting all along to take over Winterfield's operations. Together they killed her husband and they are just using us to find Winterfield. Now with Winterfield pissing everybody off and trying to steal the money himself, his so-called partners are all trying to kill him too. His stepdaughter-in-law, the mob, and some dirty politicians are chasing him. Our little gang is the bait. All these groups are using us to pull him out of hiding."

Standing up erect and very proud of myself, I feel as if I'm ten feet tall. This is a pretty impressive bunch and I solved the case.

Julie is the first to rise from the bench. She makes her way to me, for a kiss of congratulations I assume. As she pulls me close, I feel like Superman.

She whispers in my ear, "She's his daughter." She turns to the staring crowd. "Can I get anyone more coffee?"

I feel like a float in Macy's Thanksgiving parade that just ran into a light post and the air suddenly escaped.

"He's got that glazed look on his face. His theory sounded good to me," Phillip states.

Julie comes back with more coffee. She stands next to me. "I see by the look on his face that he did not tell you. Jennifer is Winterfield's daughter, or at least his stepdaughter. We think she's the money behind his construction business." Seeing that she had everyone's attention, she continues. "When his wife died twenty years ago, Jennifer inherited most of her mom's money. Most of it was held in trust accounts. After college, Jennifer gave a lot of money to him to help with his fledging construction company. They had a falling out when she started dating the son of his new wife. She and Thomas got married, and Jennifer and Winterfield did not see eye-to-eye. Then she started having an affair with Martelli. She blamed her father for her husband and his partner's construction problems. This, of course, would lead us to believe that she is after him, but when her husband was killed, she started being very friendly to Winterfield again. She hired you under the premise that she did not trust Winterfield and wanted to find Martelli because she loved him. We think that might have been true, but she was more worried about Martelli talking to the police and telling them about Winterfield's operation, which she now knew was making a ton of money."

I'm very impressed, since I got shot down with my theory, I'm glad it was by her.

Captain Jim stands up and walks toward Julie and me with his empty cup in his hand, the handle dangling from his finger. He pulls both our heads toward his. "It's not his daughter. Winterfield is a CIA plant. Jennifer's real father and mother were killed in an accident when she was a baby. Winterfield needed a family for his cover assignment, and we gave him one. He then married

Thomas Degan's mom. Thomas was already in prep school, so he was never around to meet Jennifer at that time. They met after he came home from college one year. He's been our go-between for the mob and politicians in Washington. The construction thing got out of hand, and Winterfield got so damn rich he became uncontrollable. The people he was watching became his partners. We could not pull him back. He is a renegade with money, power, and friends in the right places."

Jim goes off for his coffee.

Caruso blurts out, "Now what?"

"It seems that our friend Winterfield is not who the FBI thinks he is. He's a CIA plant."

"Would anyone like to hear what Naval Intelligence thinks?" Forester chimes in.

Jim has returned with his coffee and is standing right next to Julie and me. He knows his story is about to get shot down. Or at least a few holes will appear.

"Our mystery friend Winterfield has been used to keep track of some third world countries that looked primed for a new leader if you get my drift. We allowed his gambling operation to continue as long as he gave vital information regarding some third-world leaders that he has befriended who have become big investors in his island gambling operations. We're talking about drug money and arms money. We were using his operation to take money from these countries with no return on their investment. These so-called leaders thought they had a good pipeline into boatloads of money, but when no money floated back into their little countries, these dictators lost face with their people and we started the takeover process."

Joe has a puzzled look on his face, and Forrester turned to address him. "See, son, if these dictators keep investing their illicit funds with Winterfield, certain people in their country will be looking for a new fund manager to watch over their retirement account."

Caruso gets up and walks toward Jim, Julie, and me. Everybody holds their breath at once, thinking <u>here we go again</u>. He passes us and we let out a breath that would extinguish a blowtorch.

Forester has had enough. "Look, guys, I'm glad to help, but I have a retirement to think about. I don't care about some guy who has tricked the United States and taken the government's money for years. Jamaica, I'll help out where I can. You have my cell number, correct?"

I nod yes.

"Good. In another week or so, I won't have the Navy to help bail you guys out. I don't know what you're solving but do it quickly. This Winterfield guy is causing a lot of trouble. My experience with guys like this and the people who are chasing him is that they usually end up missing, themselves, right?"

With that, Forester shakes everyone's hand and walks out, leaving just the six of us to figure out our next step.

Just as I finish my thought, Caruso starts pacing. I felt this coming. "What do we have here? Is this a case or a wild goose chase? I'm not sure we really can do anything else down here."

Joe decides to step to the plate. "Since we're here, why don't we at least use some contacts to see if anything else is brewing? Why can't Miss FBI call her people and see if Winterfield has surfaced anywhere? Dad, why don't you call home and speak to your shady friends? I'm sure their network of contacts is better than we have right now."

"What about me, General?" Caruso asked, attempting humor.

"I think you and Phillip should secure our passage to one of the outer islands. I have a feeling that will be our next stop."

I'm very impressed. "Why do you think that?"

"While we were on the cutter, I heard the Navy Captain talking on his cell phone with Uncle Bill. The Captain was pretty much yessing Uncle Bill to death, but he did mention that it would be better if a certain someone went back to his island and did not surface for a while."

"Let's head back to the motel. Julie, can we drop you somewhere?"

"I'll stick around if you don't mind. Your son is very smart. I'll gladly call my office and see what's up. I feel used. They owe me."

That's a line I didn't want to touch, at least not yet.

CHAPTER TWENTY-ONE

VISITORS FROM NEW YORK

As we leave the mess hall, two drivers are waiting to take us wherever we need to go, as long as it's away from the base. Orders from Forester. All our gear seems to be here. We all forgot our very expensive fishing stuff. Part of our five-hundred-dollar-a-day habit. The trip through town is spent in silent contemplation and wet, smelly clothes. We could use a shower. Usually, a drive down Duval Street would start some reminiscing about the good old days, but now it brings just blank stares as we all wonder if we're in over our heads.

It seems like no time before we arrive at our motel. I thank the drivers. We grab our rods and walk to our rooms. I walk off to the lobby to see if there are any messages. There are plenty. Caruso and Phillip head for their room. Captain Jim is standing around, looking lost. We left his van back at the dock. Oops. I offer to call him a cab, but he would like to assist us. He goes to the lobby and gets a room for himself. Julie is without money, identification, credit cards, or anything. I forgot we pulled her off the boat when we dove in. She'll have to stay with us. What a shame.

Joe, Julie, and I walk down the sidewalk toward our room. The sun is going down and, no matter how many times you see it, you can't help staring. From our lovely motel, we get a decent view. It's not Mallory Square, but it will do. Julie and I stare in silence until the sun falls behind the parking garage. Joe turns and opens the door.

"Dad."

I turn to see Uncle Gino sitting on the bed. He's not alone. Backing him up are the two biggest redwood trees I've ever seen.

Gino barks "Close the door."

Gino very rarely raises his tone of voice. This is not going to be good. He looks like he's been forced out of retirement. I pull Julie into our tiny phone booth of a room. As soon as we close the door, there is a knock. I open it with permission from Uncle Gino. The tree trunks have their hands in their jackets. Captain Jim has come to see if everything is okay. He heard the infamous Gino bark through the paper-thin walls that separate our rooms.

Now we're crowded.

Another knock on the door and Gino waves me to open it. This time it's Caruso and Phillip.

"I was getting ice when I saw Jim coming to your room. It looked funny. Hello Gino," Caruso offers awkwardly.

This is starting to resemble the stateroom scene from The Marx Brothers 'Night at the Opera'. All we need now is the chambermaid and the engineer to come in. There are nine people crowded around two tiny beds.

Gino is getting more and more aggravated by the second.

"We need to talk," Gino looks at the mass of people trying to look innocent.

"Shall we clear the room boss?" Tree Trunk One says.

"Jamaica, can we trust them?"

I look at Julie and Jim. I dare not reveal their identities. Gino would have me killed on the spot, well maybe not killed but at least very hurt by the two frozen slabs of dumb. "Yes, I trust them."

Gino gets up. He tries to walk to me but everybody must step out of the way. What a sight.

Gino whispers, "I need to find Winterfield. I need him alive. This is my life we're talking about. Some friends of mine have turned against us. They want Winterfield for themselves. I want him alive, and these so-called <u>friends</u> of mine are out of the picture. I don't care what happens to them. Do you get the picture? If I get Winterfield back on track and away from certain people, everything will be okay. I'm getting pressure from all over. *I will not go to jail because of this!*" His voice ends in a mild roar.

With that Gino and the beef walkout, or at least try to. They have to squeeze around us, which reduces the dramatic effect of their departure.

As the door slams shut, I look around the room. "I suppose you all heard that?"

Everybody nods sheepishly. "Did anybody understand it?" I ask.

"I was ready to call it quits, but with Uncle Gino asking a favor in his way, it's hard to walk away," Caruso lends a thought.

"Do we wonder why?" Joe asks.

Julie interrupts, "I'm going to check in and see what my people know. From what I have seen and heard, we are the last to get information. It's worth a shot."

I point to the phone. "Do you want privacy?"

"After letting me stay for that last conversation, I owe you one."

Julie walks over to the nightstand and picks up the phone. The motel operator gets her a connection. It goes right through; must be a local call.

Julie explains what has been going on, but does not bring up the fact that we are with her or anything about Uncle Gino. Smart girl. For about three minutes she listens intently. Finally, she ends the conversation. "I'm going to stick around for a few more days. I'll need a survival kit. I left everything on the boat when I bailed out. Thanks." She hangs up.

Julie turns to us. "It seems that Winterfield has double-crossed everybody he's worked with. This gambling operation has gotten quite large. It's run from one of the outer private islands of the Bahamas. It seems he has pissed off a Saudi prince who's given him some front money to start up an operation for overseas gamblers in the Mid East. He took some more money from some mob guys and gave it to the prince to give the impression that this operation is making money. He's moving so much money that he's not concentrating on the gambling business. The problem is, the operation has not started yet, so he has the prince pissed at him for lying. I guess the prince has morals, and these mob guys are out all this money. The prince tried to take back his investment, but Winterfield wired the money into another person's account in the Cayman Islands."

"Let me guess: Jennifer Degan," I interject proudly as if I've found the missing link.

"Not exactly." There's a pause as she looks at me. "Try a fellow by the name of Jamaica Biltmore."

Not in a million years would I ever suspect that Winterfield would use me like this. I don't know if I should be flattered or furious. What happens if I get to the money before he does? Is it mine? Talk about a moral dilemma. "How much are we talking about?"

"Let's say in the neighborhood of one-point-eight billion dollars."

"That's some neighborhood." This is about all I could come up with. "All right gang, let's put the money issue aside. Where do we go from here?"

I look at everyone. I don't see a thought swirling around anyone's head. I guess it'll be up to me again to figure out our next move. Well, we're all snuggled in my little room and it's time for some fresh air. "How about some dinner on Duval Street?" I offer.

"I'm going to have to get back to New York City tomorrow," Caruso says. "What about Sloppy Joe's for a bite? At least the Hemingway stuff is cool.".

I forgot that he's only down here for a few days. We're going to miss him. There's a knock on the door. I make my way through the crowd and open the door. It's the desk manager. "Mr. Biltmore, you said there would not be more than two people in your room. This looks like a lot more than two."

"We all have rooms here. What can I do for you?" The manager hands me a phone message and turns and walks away. I close the door and read it. I chuckle to myself.

"What is it, Dad?"

"It seems our lovely client would like to meet on one of the outer islands of the Bahamas. What do we think?"

"It's a trap."

"How did she know you were here?"

"I wouldn't go."

"I'm coming with you."

I look around the room, trying to figure out who said what.

Caruso waves his hand. "Wait a minute. Since she knew you were here, she easily could have tried to kill us. Why drag us to someplace where we would be expecting something to happen?"

Good reasoning.

Captain Jim chimes in, "Right now we are in the U.S.A., and the investigation's proceeding pretty well, especially when you have a cop and an FBI agent involved. Put us on an island where this guy Winterfield owns the government, and bodies can disappear and nobody cares."

Silence. "James Bond never had trouble in the Bahamas." I hate when these things slip out. I was thinking it, but I never really wanted to say it.

"I say we go. I'll get a plane to take us. Jamaica, you inform Forester where we're going. Jim, you, Joe and Caruso take another plane and meet us there. If we all show up on one plane and this is a surprise attack, we'll be in for it," Phillip suggests.

"What about me?" asks Julie.

"I think you should go with Jamaica and me." God, I love that guy.

I can see Caruso thinking. "That's not bad Phillip. How did you come up with it?"

"I didn't want to say this before, but some of this is right out of my last book."

"Do we make it home?" I try to break the tension.

"Most of us do. Only kidding."

The Captain interjects, "I think we'll need some weapons, or at least Caruso, Julie, and I do. You're dangerous Biltmore."

Finally, Joe laughs. Right about now, his head is spinning like Linda Blair in the Exorcist.

"Let's meet at Sloppy Joe's in one hour." The gang splits up. Everybody heads back to their room. It's time for Joe and me to shower and dress for dinner. I'm sure we'll play twenty questions before we leave.

CHAPTER TWENTY-TWO

WOULD HEMINGWAY GO?

Joe and I get dressed in silence. Joe says he's going for ice while I finish up in the bathroom. I try to call Phillip to tell him we're running a couple of minutes late. The phone is dead, so I head over to his room, knowing Joe has a key. I open the door and look for Joe by the ice machine – no Joe. I walk down the outside corridor and knock on Phillip's door. No answer. I head back to my room. Should I check in on Julie? Nah. I walk back into my room. The bathroom door is closed. Joe must be finishing up. I know that if I asked how he was doing we'd never go out for dinner, and I'm starving. But I need to know. Things here are getting a little scary, and I don't need him being scared.

I hold my breath and talk through the bathroom door, "Tell me what you're thinking."

No answer. I hate when he gets mad. He clams up. I better do the talking. "If you're worried, I understand. This is getting above me too. Am I scared? (Not really but it can't hurt.) A little, but we have good people on our side. Do I trust the CIA guy? I'm not sure. Julie, we can trust, I hope; plus she's pretty. Phillip did come up with a good plan, right? Come on, Joe, you have to give me something to work with. If this is too much, you need to tell me now and you can wait here; I really will understand. I'd be a little worried too if I were you. I mean, this guy has tried to kill us a couple of times and, if it weren't for some quick thinking, we'd be dead, which is not a good thought. I'm glad Caruso isn't going home for another day, plus when you think about it, Forester will be looking out for us no matter what he says. I can't believe he won't be around the corner waiting to help when we scream for it, not that we'll scream for it or even need it, but you never know. Joe, I need to know what the hell you're thinking about, or else I'll send you off to college tomorrow."

With that, the door to the room opens and Joe walks in with the ice bucket and Julie in tow. I hate talking to an empty bathroom, especially when I'll have to do this all over again. He looks numb.

"Dad, I have to ask you something. With all the people you know all over the world, did you set this whole thing up to give me some thrills? Because, if you did, I think it's working. Yes, it's a little scary, but overall I'm getting into it. I'll go get the others."

With that, he leaves Julie and me alone. "Let me guess, you're trying to get your son hooked up in your line of work? Mr. Biltmore!" She offers as she closes the door.

I didn't need another lecture. It's time for dinner. I walk past Julie to open the door.

"This is between Joe and me. I want him with me. He's all I got."

With that, she pulls me to her and kisses me. "I didn't want to wait until you made the first move. You look like the slow type."

Julie has shocked me. She continues, "I understand with your son; I was only asking. I can help make things more exciting, but I think you have that in hand."

With that, she turns and leaves me in the room by myself. Now that was great, but my mind is cloudy. Talk about having your stars in alignment! We have Joe getting into the case, Julie getting into a semi-good plan, a night, and me on Duval Street in Key West. I walk into the outside corridor that separates the parking lot from the rooms and to the lobby where my gang is waiting. If we can get through dinner without anybody trying to kill us, it will be a perfect night. We start walking in pairs to Duval Street from a side street. Phillip and Jim are leading the pack. Julie and Joe are next, and Caruso and I are bringing up the rear.

"You have a dazed look on your face. What's going on?" Caruso inquires.

"I've just got a lot on my mind. I'm a little worried about Joe." I point with my chin to Julie. "What do you think about Julie?"

"I've seen that look before. Could you at least wait until the case is over before you fall for her? You get all foggy when you fall for a girl. Now is not the time for this."

"I'll be fine. Let's just have a nice dinner and see what else Phillip has for us. What do you make of his statement that some of this stuff is from his books?"

"I'm sure he thinks it is. All those mystery novel writers have the same stuff in their books. There are just so many ideas you can make up," Caruso explains.

We have arrived at Sloppy Joe's. We all pile in the long, narrow, dark bar. I can't help but look at all the Hemingway pictures on the wall. I look at Hemingway and Fuentes standing next to the Pilar, which was probably loaded up with guns, whiskey, and fishing poles, as they are about to embark on an adventure in the Caribbean looking for German submarines. I look over at my bunch and wonder if we look that exciting to an outsider. I shake my head: Definitely not.

We get seated right away at a wooden table right next to the bar. Everyone orders a drink, even Joe. That's okay with me. The waiter brings a menu and we don't seem to notice. Phillip has our attention.

"We can leave tomorrow morning. I have two seaplanes set up. We fly one plane into Total Cay as instructed, and the other plane will land at Cinco Cay. This is a public island about one mile from Total Cay, which is privately owned. Let's say it should have been called Paradise Island, but the name was taken."

Julie responds first. "Getting somewhere is always the easy part of a plan. What do we do when we get there? How do the rest of us get there? What I've heard about these private islands is that security is tighter than at the White House."

My turn. "Some of us don't need to surprise them. They're expecting us. They know we're all together. I'm sure they're expecting us to stay together. Caruso, you make reservations to head back home first thing in the morning and head out, all packed up. I'll make a scene with Julie in the morning as if she's headed back to FBI headquarters. Jim, you disappear into the woodwork. Phillip will accompany me to Total Cay by plane with

Joe. I have a funny feeling we're being set up. You have to give the guy credit: Putting the money in my name takes guts. I think we'll need a couple of weapons for protection."

Julie chimes in. "I'll handle that. We can find stuff that is untraceable. Will you call Forester?"

"Without a doubt; he's not retired yet. We'll milk him for whatever he's worth."

We order dinner and another round of drinks. I have learned over the years that after two drinks, any type of planning is useless.

Julie asks about how we all came together. I explain about Caruso and me growing up together on Long Island. Phillip decides he will handle his own stories. After his second glass of burgundy, you'd think he was Ernst Hemingway himself. I mean, Phillip's books did well, but they do not compare with 'Islands in the Stream' or 'To Have or Have Not.'

Dinner ends with an espresso. It's been a long day. We all had plans to do the town, but the conversation seems to be waning except for Phillip. I don't think Jim has said three words all night. Joe has been quiet too. Phillip pays the bill and we head out onto Duval Street, which is hopping; I wish I could say that for us. We slowly walk back toward our motel in silence; it's a combination of being plumb tired and feeling nervous about tomorrow. Jim, Phillip, and Caruso bid us good night. We'll catch up in the morning and start the plan going. Joe walks ahead to our room and just waves good night to everyone. I'll talk with him later; he needs it.

Julie has that look in her eye. "Do you want to come in and let me know what kind of weapons we need?"

What a line. On one hand, I have Julie asking me in, and on the other hand, I have Joe probably scared out of his wits. "Anything you come up with will be fine, the smaller the better." I could kick myself. Now it's my turn. I lean over and kiss her good night. I try mumbling something about Joe and walk off.

I open the door to my room and Joe is already in bed with the TV on. "I wasn't expecting you so soon. You know, Dad, this will be great tomorrow. I have a good feeling about this. When you look at things, we've been handling them pretty well. I know you can't shoot very well but, with Jim and Caruso, I think we have a good chance. What do you think Jennifer wants? Do you think Winterfield is with her?"

I just stand at the foot of the bed: To think I just passed up a night with Julie to listen to Joe talk as if he's a rat on crack! That's the last time I let him have a double espresso right before bedtime. I head for the bathroom as Joe drones on and on. I'm back and getting into bed and he doesn't miss a beat. I'm afraid to go to sleep. Joe will never sleep, and he'll be useless tomorrow. I figure it's time for a lecture; it'll bore him and knock him out, or at least me, either one will be fine.

CHAPTER TWENTY-THREE

ISLAND HOPPING

I don't have to tell any boring stories for Joe to fall asleep. Sleep comes quickly to him. I wish I could say the same for myself. My head is spinning all night. I see sunrise trying to get into my room through the non-room darkening shades. I slowly dress. There is a soft knock on the door. I open slowly, not expecting much but hoping for the world. No luck. Standing outside with two cups of hot coffee is Caruso. He knows my habits; they're like him: when we're traveling we tend to rise early, usually for fishing. Today the fishing will be of another nature. Not wanting to disturb Joe, I walk outside to witness a wonderful sight, sunrise in Key West. I take the coffee from Caruso. I take a long slug from the Styrofoam cup and let the caffeine surge through my veins.

"How'd he do last night?"

"He's great. He's getting into this case. He rambled on and on and finally bored himself so much he fell asleep early. I was up most of the night. What about you?"

Caruso looks as tired as I feel. "I'll be glad to go back to work and get some rest. Are you worried about today? I mean you, Phillip, and Joe are closer to Moe, Larry, and Curly than to Sherlock Holmes, Watson, and Indiana Jones, if you get my point"

I did not have the heart to tell him that this was the exact reason I was up all night.

"I know I'm better off with Phillip's plan, but I want Joe with me. I think he'll do great."

God, I miss my guns. On cue, Caruso raises his tee shirt to expose both my beloved pistols. I lovingly take them and place them in my waistband, covering them with my tee-shirt. Security.

"I figured you'd need these sooner or later." I don't need to reply. "Phillip and Jim are out already. Getting the planes I surmise. Have you knocked on Julie's door?"

"Not yet."

"Be careful with her. You need to keep your head clear. This is not a New York City case any longer. There's some strange stuff going on here, and you seem to be right in the middle of it. It's as if this whole thing was planned to suck you in and use you to get the money."

"I'm a cautious type of guy. I'll call Forester and call in one more favor. I might need the whole Navy to back us up. Let's get our plan going. Start packing to leave and I'll get Julie to do the same."

"I hope this works." Caruso does not sound overly optimistic as he leaves to check out of the motel.

If somebody is watching, I better start acting the part. I call after Caruso, "Have a good flight. Stop into my place and make sure Bobby's doing OK. I'm going to say goodbye to Julie."

Caruso acts his part out and waves. I head to Julie's door. She walks out with her bag in hand.

"Heading back to work?" I offer. Hopefully, somebody is listening to make this all worthwhile. I get a strange thought: what if our Miss Julie is our little informant. Nah.

"Yes, give me a call if anything pops up."

We have that awkward silence as we stare at each other. Now it's my turn. I kiss her.

"How did it go with Joe? Is he okay?"

"Better than okay," I say aloud. I then whisper, "Any luck with getting a weapon or two?"

"I have a contact meeting me soon," is all Julie will say.

A taxicab pulls up to the motel. Julie has played this part well. "Call me." She gets in and the taxi pulls away.

Two down. I'm sure Jim is already gone; I don't need to check. Joe and Phillip converge on me at the same time. Time to fly.

I turn to Phillip, "Where do we pick up the plane?"

"Key West International —kind of. I had to pull some strings. They usually don't have seaplanes taking off anymore," Phillip offers.

A cab pulls up and we get in. Phillip, Joe, and I ride silently through the dark streets toward the airport. God, I want to see Key West again. Phillip, who is seated in the front seat, points the driver away from the terminals. We head toward the rear of the airport, toward the waterside; makes sense. We pull up to the closed chain-link fence. A security guard who is responsible for stopping people from leaving our country opens the gate with a nod and a smile. The driver looks at Phillip who points to the dock with our seaplane tied up to it. I flew in one of these contraptions only once in my life and swore I would never do this again. Runways should not go up and down. Most pilots have trouble with flat ones, never mind ones that heave like a roller coaster out of control. This will be no fun. The pilot, who is faceless due to the dark windows, starts the twin radial engines. We take our gear from the cab, pay the driver, and head for the dock. Something is fishy about the steward who takes our bags, but something is familiar about him.

We head up the gangplank toward the plane. I'm followed first by Joe and then by Phillip. I'm so glad Caruso gave me my guns. We're the only ones on the Grumman Albatross, an ancient flying boat. Flying boat — what an oxymoron. As we sit down in the plane our pilot comes out of his cabin. I see the door handle slowly open, and I reach for my guns as Admiral Forester walks out with a huge smile on his face.

"Did you think I was going to let my Godchild go with you alone? Plus, I could use some flying hours to keep my certification up."

"Can you fly one of these things?" I ask in wonder.

"I have driven a boat and flown a fighter jet, how hard can it be to combine the two?" Forester asks straight-faced.

He does not see that I can see right into the cabin. Thank goodness I notice someone seated in the pilot's seat. I would have jumped off and swam to the Bahamas if I thought for one moment that he was taking us.

From the cabin, "Sir, we're cleared for take-off."

"Sit back; we'll be there in forty minutes. We've checked ahead and told the island that we must stick around for you to get back into the country without a problem. They bought it." Forester throws me a little black key chain that resembles a remote car lock. "Just hit this and we'll be there."

Very cool. I slip it into my pocket. Forester goes back into the cabin. I figure, with so little flying time, we better formulate a plan. Over the roar of the engines and the splashing of the water, I try to stay calm and talk with Joe and Phillip.

"All right, guys. I'm sure we'll be greeted when we get there. They're not going to let us walk around a private island. I hope that Jennifer will be part of our welcoming committee." I hand Joe one of my guns and he takes it without protest. "Keep it hidden," I instruct him. "Phillip, do you have anything?"

Phillip shows me his nine-millimeter Baretta tucked into his waistband.

"Guys, I think we're going to wing it. Let's try not to get cornered. Stay together and try to stay in the open where Forester can keep an eye on us."

As I talk, I hear the unmistakable sound of the engines winding down, indicating that we're coming in for a landing. Make that a splashdown. Picture yourself as an ice cube being dropped into a glass of water from two feet away; that's what a seaplane landing feels like. I can't help but look out the window at the water cascading down the window from the force of our landing. I just pray that I don't see a lot of bubbles and sea life passing by the window. The water leaves the window faster than a window washer with a squeegee on Tenth Avenue on a summer day. I look over and Joe has his head buried into the vomit bag, losing his breakfast. I reach over to pat his back, reassuring him we have landed okay. Forester walks from the cabin and sees the green pale of Joe's face.

"Sorry about that. We tried to make it a smooth landing, but a few waves interrupted our pattern."

"There's no such thing as a smooth landing with one of these things."

Forester leans over the seat to me, "Stay close, They won't allow us out of the plane. They don't trust us either. Joe, you okay?"

Joe looks up from the bag. "Fine."

Through the window, I can see someone on the dock waiting to throw us a tie line. The boat—plane pulls closer, the pilot kills the engines, and the real captain comes from the cabin, opens the door, and catches the line. I walk to the hatch. Looks like a deep-water dock, which will make it very interesting to get off this thing. Just then a small twelve-foot rubber inflatable makes its way to us. I motion for Joe and Phillip to get in first, which they do.

I turn to Forester. "I hope my backup crew is somewhere within the same ocean."

"I have the Coast Guard standing by. Just hit the button."

Chapter Twenty-Four

Some Call It Paradise

I make my way off the boat and into the bright sunshine. I survey the area. This would be one hell of a vacation spot if it weren't for the killers lurking about. The dock, a long wooden runway about one hundred feet long, is completely deserted. It leads to a small cabana sitting on the sand by itself. From here it looks like the only thing on this island is the dock and the cabana. There are plenty of palm trees circling the cabin and the rest of the beachfront. Off in the distance is an island that looks to be about the size of a postage stamp. I see something that resembles a boat motoring back and forth along its shoreline, hopefully, Caruso and company.

We get off the boat and our driver motions us up the dock towards the cabana. He takes off, not a good sign. Then, from the cabana, I see Jennifer and someone else walking toward us. She is waving. The gentleman doesn't look familiar.

"Who is that?" asks Joe.

"Beats me," is about all I have in me.

They're walking toward us, which I take as a good sign and not a trick. We'll meet about halfway up the dock. Jennifer, dressed in a light sundress, and the gentleman, who looks forty and fit and is wearing shorts, tee-shirt, flip flops, a wide-brimmed straw hat, and smoking a cigar the size of my forearm, look very happy to see us.

"Mr. Biltmore, it's nice to kind of see you again. I'm sorry I don't know your son's name."

"Joe and this is Phillip," I give up. "And you are?" Holding my breath.

"Robert Martelli, Mr. Biltmore. Nice to meet you."

Chevy Chase couldn't do a double-take any better. Joe and Phillip are staring at Martelli. I want to act like Moe and poke them both in the eyes.

Jennifer laughs. "Surprised?"

Trying to hide my surprise, "Nothing surprises me anymore about this case."

"Follow us, Mr. Biltmore, and we'll try and explain," beckons Martelli. I don't want to.

"Look, we've been on that plane for a while. I'm wondering if we could talk out here for a little. Joe got sick on the plane, and the fresh air will do him good."

"I know what you mean. I'll never ride in one of those things again." Jennifer offers in sympathy. I notice someone else moving in the cabana.

"Could we at least head inside for a cool drink?" Martelli offers as our host. He sees me staring at the cabana. "Don't worry, Mr. Biltmore. This is not a set-up. We need you, not unlike Mr. Winterfield, who would rather you go away."

With that, Jennifer and Martelli turn and head for the cabana. My two companions and I pause and look at each other for guidance. I glance over my shoulder for support from Forester who is probably looking at me but, with the sun's glare, I don't see anything.

We decide to follow. I calculate our odds. Even if there is someone in the cabana, we have three guns, three people, lots of bullets, and absolutely no experience in this type of stuff whatsoever.

"Put your sunglasses on," I tell my gang.

"Why, Dad?"

"Son, after being in this sunlight, when we walk into the darkened cabana we won't be able to see for a second or two. That'll be enough time for a surprise attack. Let's catch up with our guests. I don't need them disappearing once they get into the cabana and we're hit by some over-sized henchmen." This is about all I can think of. We quicken our pace and arrive at the cabana right behind Jennifer and Martelli.

Martelli opens the door and holds it for us. I decide to let ladies go first, so I motion for Jennifer to lead the way, which she does without hesitating. The coolness of the cabana is overwhelming. The room is no larger than a good-sized hotel suite. There is one room, a bedroom off to one side, a bathroom in the rear, and a living room in the middle. The whole place is decorated in early Miami Vice, pastel colors everywhere. A houseboy is operating the open bar, ready to serve. I quickly check out the entire suite on the premise of just being plain snoopy.

Martelli goes to the bar and grabs a drink from the houseboy. "What can I get you?"

Phillip looks at me. "Three beers will do fine," I answer as I finish my tour, confident that we're alone. Phillip, Joe, and I grab our beers and sit on three different couches. It's perfect planning to be separated; I wish I had thought of it, but it just worked out this way. I decide to get straight to the point.

"We are surprised to see you still alive Mr. Martelli. We've been shot at, blown up, and thrown off a boat in the past day, so forgive us if we've lost our sense of humor. It seems Winterfield has trailed us from New York to here, tried to have a speed boat run us over in the water, lured us onto his boat and tried to sink it, and, last but not least, had two jet skiers and a helicopter try to blow us out of the water."

"You must have one heck of a guardian angel, Mr. Biltmore," Martelli says as he takes a long swig of his umbrella drink. I choose to ignore him.

"Mrs. Degan, how long did you two plan out this little deception?"

Jennifer looks at Martelli. "You wouldn't believe it if I told you, but here goes. Robert set this up himself. I came down here looking for Winterfield, and Robert was down here looking to avenge Thomas's death. Am I glad he's still alive? Yes. Did we plan this? No. Mr. Biltmore, I do not need your approval or permission to do this. We want your help. This island belongs to my family. Winterfield set up a small but high-class casino on the other side of the island and has been profiting from it ever since. We have been holed up here for the last two days, hoping he'd show up. My contacts spotted you getting off the plane in Florida and followed you. My family still has many friends down here. I know you do too. We feel Winterfield had Thomas killed and is swindling money from every crooked politician, third-world dictator, and mobster looking to make a quick buck. My proposition to you is this: with your resources, help us find Winterfield. Do what you will with him, and you and your group will receive a finder's fee of one million dollars. From what I've seen of your operation, Mr. Biltmore, you could use the money. We'll expect an answer from you in twenty-four hours. Just call this number."

Jennifer hands me a card. We rise. We shake hands with Martelli. We put our beers down and head into the open sunlight. Forester sees us coming and is waiting to untie the plane from the dock.

We make our way up the long dock. I never like turning my back on someone, and I can feel Jennifer and Martelli right behind me. In the distance, I see a motorboat slowly heading toward us. A little gun shy now, I stare at it until it comes into view. Forester, Phillip, and Joe seem frozen in time. We're all expecting the worst.

Forester yells to the pilot, "Start the engines; we might have to leave quickly."

From the bow of the boat, I see Julie waving. We all let out a sigh of relief. We could use a break from the shooting.

Curiosity makes me turn around to see what our hosts are up to. The sound of the motorboat and the engines starting on the seaplane has drowned out the sound of a golf cart picking up Martelli and Jennifer. I watch them get in, Martelli notices me watching and waves. The driver takes them further into the woods and they disappear. I feel a little better. I turn and watch Jim maneuver the boat right past the plane and dock right where we're standing – showoff. Julie throws me a line as Phillip leans over and pulls on the rail.

"Well? How did it go?" Caruso asks. I wait for Jim to cut his engines. Forester motions to the pilot of the seaplane to cut his.

"We've learned in this case to expect the unexpected. It seems our client does want our help, and her partner agrees." I figure I'll let that dangle for a second to see who'll bite.

"Partner?" I knew it would be Caruso.

"Our bridge jumper, Robert Martelli." With that, you could hear the snappers scurrying around the dock looking for their lunch.

"I know this doesn't mean much, but we have our first crime," Caruso lets out. "That's a no-no to the New York City Police."

He's right; it's not going to mean much.

"What's our next step?" Joe asks. We have enough brainpower to come up with a good answer. I look around at the experience assembled on the dock: FBI, CIA, police, writer, and Navy Admiral. These are some of the best criminal investigative minds I've seen. Surely they'll figure out our next step. Most people who are experts in their field need to process the thought before talking, unlike me. I see everyone fumbling for their thoughts. I see Jim about to step up to the plate. Good, here we go.

"I need to find a real paying customer; if you guys need me any further, Phillip can track me down." That was no help.

Caruso cuts in, "I got a call from New York, and I need to get the first flight back." No help here.

"This is not Navy business. I have a fleet to prepare for. They're returning from six months in South America, and it's my last review before sailing into retirement." That's three swings and not even a foul ball. Next.

"I'm open to suggestions, but I'll have to check in with headquarters, and I'm sure they'll re-assign me," Julie offers. Next batter. I look at my last two hopes, Phillip and Joe.

"You know me; I have nothing to do. I'd like to fish while we're down here but, if we don't, no big deal." I didn't figure I'd get a whole lot from Phillip. My last hope is Joe.

"We could look at a couple of colleges while we're down here. The weather is nice; I could get used to this."

I shake my head. "I can't believe what I'm hearing. Is everybody giving up? Did Columbus give up when he was at sea for three months without land? Did George Washington give up when the weather got cold in Valley Forge and the English were breathing down his neck? Did Churchill give up when the Germans were bombing London day in and day out? Did Moe give up when Larry and Curly screwed up all the time?"

With that, Forester gets the pilot to start the engines and starts shaking everybody's hand. Jim returns to the cockpit of the boat and starts his engines.

"Dad, if you don't mind, I'd rather go back by boat."

"Okay, see you back at the hotel."

"Are we checking out?" Joe asks.

"I don't know; I forgot about Gino and his request. I'm going to head back with Forester. Does anybody else want a ride?" I offer.

"I'll come back with you," Julie says as she gets off the boat. I see Caruso looking at me. So there we have it:

Joe, Jim, Caruso, and Phillip get seated on the boat. I untie the bowline. Forester and I push off and the boat heads back to Key West. Forester walks ahead of us up the gangplank into the plane. Julie goes next and I follow. I give one last turn to see if we're being watched. I always think we are. I stare into the cabana. It's probably just my personality, but I feel like I see somebody watching us. Oh well. Time to head back and re-group, even if the group is Joe and Phillip. I never need help anyway. It always comes down to me and that's why I like doing what I do. It's the lone wolf mentality. I enter the plane and look at Julie who is seated already. Her eyes are closed and she's falling asleep. Damn, it would be fun having her around. This lone wolf stuff sucks.

Forester closes the door as I take a seat next to Julie.

CHAPTER TWENTY-FIVE

BACK TO BASICS

The plane ride back is uneventful, which means no one throws up. Suddenly a bad thought creeps into my brain. With all the people after us, I should be on the boat with the rest of the gang. I tell myself Joe will be fine with Caruso there.

The landing at the hands of Forester is a lot better than I guessed it would be. We taxi for only a minute and then dock. Forester is the first one out of the cabin. He has a sheepish smile on his face as if it was his first time and he's proud. Forester bids us farewell. I thank him for the backup. I'm sure I have not seen the last of him on this case. Julie and I take the short trip back to the motel. She explains that she has all her stuff at the dock in Jim's van. I'd forgotten that she even checked out of the room. This will get awkward when we get back; it's like dating again.

"Where are we headed?" she asks.

"Back to the motel to plan out my next move. It seems everyone wants me to find Winterfield now. I don't know what the case is all about anymore. Would you like me to drop you somewhere?" (Hopefully not.)

"I'll tag along for a while Could we call Caruso and have him retrieve my things and bring them back to the motel? I'll stay with you if you don't mind until I help sort this thing out. I'll have to head back to work in the morning though."

"I'll call Caruso. What a wonderful thought. I can check up on the gang."

Julie hands me her cell phone and I call Caruso. They are about thirty minutes from the dock and will head over after they get in. Caruso has arranged to take the late flight out of Fort Lauderdale. Jim will disappear into the woodwork, and Joe and I will plan our next move. The taxi drops us off at the motel. I pay the driver and slowly walk towards my room.

"What time will they be back?" Julie asks.

This is one of those date questions. "About one hour," I answer sheepishly. My mind is in the gutter right now.

Julie slips her hand in mine as I unlock the door. I have that warm fuzzy feeling inside. I'm relaxed and try to act as cool as possible. One whole hour to escape from this craziness. I lead Julie into the dark cool room. I notice a lone figure standing in the corner. I pull away from Julie and slam the door.

"Damn it, Winterfield, how did you get in here?"

Chapter Twenty-Six

Confessions Of A Mad Man

Winterfield looks like a man running for his life. Maybe we can put some of the puzzle together. Phillip and Joe will not be back for an hour, so we can use this time to sort things out. I had other plans for this hour, but this will have to do.

"I need help. Biltmore, you seem to have the right connections to put a stop to those trying to kill me," Winterfield blurts out.

I look at Julie who still has that dumbstruck look on her face.

"Is she okay?" Winterfield begs.

"She's fine. I'm sure there's something she'll be able to do to help. I have a ton of questions. Certain things don't add up. While we were out on the ocean, who was trying to kill us? You were on your boat? I haven't pieced that together yet. Why would you try to kill us and invite us on your boat at the same time? I realize that you did try to kill us later when you blew up your own boat. And again, while we were heading back to Key West, we were attacked but you would not have known we were still alive after you tried to blow us up." Boy, that was a lot to get out, and I'm not sure it made sense.

Winterfield paces the small room. I notice his clothes are not the neatly pressed type that we are used to seeing him in. He's been living in these clothes for a day or so. Julie sits on one of the beds. I think Winterfield is trying to figure out an answer to my convoluted question.

"Much to my dismay, there are people protecting me whether I want it or not. Everyone who comes near me gets greeted like that."

"Let's get into your background. Who are you, really? In the last few days we've heard you are everything from an FBI plant to an ex-CIA agent to an employee for the United States Government. You're a smart fellow, but you're not crazy enough to try and deceive everybody."

"Put it this way: I'm a free agent. Or at least I was. I now need your help. You seem to have a full complement of people willing to help you. I am now a target of a full assault on me and my operations. I want to trust you Mr. Biltmore, but if I get double-crossed, there will be hell to pay. Whoever needs my services gets them, at my price. I use everyone and anyone to get what I want. During Vietnam, I worked counter-intelligence for all the agencies. I had contacts all over the world from a family business. My dad owned one of the largest construction companies in the world, but he had romantic thoughts of being a spy, and it ruined the business. He got killed during a raid of some sort while working for the CIA in North Africa. That's when I got involved and took over.

I was just smarter and had no notions of being a spy for the glamour of it. I was out to work all sides of the fence and make money. I consolidated the construction business into two areas, New York and Las Vegas. I stopped the spy stuff after I got married to Jennifer's mother. I was just putting this whole gambling thing together when she died. The construction business led to my contact with the mob and politicians. I tried to keep my stepson and his partner from entering my business for their own good. Yes, Thomas is my stepson and Jennifer is my stepdaughter. They had different mothers and they never really knew each other. When Thomas's mother left me, she took Thomas to live with her. Thomas and I connected again when he came to New York for college. Now I'm on the run because someone is trying to get this gambling business from me. I'm trying to protect my interest and your buddy, Gino. No matter what people say, he's been completely loyal, as long as we send him his share. It's when the politicians got involved that everyone worried about protecting themselves and covering their tracks. This is a legit business."

"What about the missing money that we've been looking for?" Julie blurts out.

Oh boy. This can't be good.

"Which agency do you work for?" Winterfield inquires.

"FBI."

"The money is safe. Your computer guys are not that good. Remember, at the end of the day, they make only thirty thousand dollars a year. They don't care that much. My guys live the best life possible, and their pay is a percent of what we pull in, sometimes in the millions."

"That's a nice incentive plan," I offer. I really can't think of anything intelligent to say. I want to talk about today's trip to the casino island and Martelli being alive, but I'm not sure how much we can trust Winterfield yet. There's a knock on the door. I motion for Winterfield to get into the bathroom. I slowly open the door.

Caruso is standing there, bags in hand. Joe and Phillip are talking in the parking lot with Jim.

"I came to say goodbye. If you need anything call. Remember, Jamaica, this is different than the stuff we face in New York," Caruso warns.

I shake his hand and nod. I notice Phillip saying goodbye to Jim: two down. Joe and Phillip walk toward me. I can't stop them. Joe walks into the room but sees Julie sitting on the bed; he's thinking bad thoughts, I can tell. Phillip walks right past me and into the room. He stops in his tracks when he sees Julie too.

I close the door. "You can come out now."

With that, Winterfield walks out of the bathroom. What a great look on Joe and Phillip's faces. I cannot review what has just transpired because I don't have that much time to explain. I need to know the next step. On one hand, I have Jennifer and Martelli still paying me to find Winterfield and, on the other hand, we have Winterfield needing my help for something.

"What do you need from me?" I need to be blunt.

"I need you to smooth things over with Gino and his people. I need to find Jennifer and explain what's going on. Lastly, I need Washington off my back. This is still a great business, Mr. Biltmore, and it's legal. I'll give you one million dollars to get this mess cleared up. There's a bank account-"

I interrupt, "In the Cayman Islands with my name on it. I heard."

" I'll leave one million dollars in there for you to do with as you wish. I have an island where there is a casino." Winterfield takes the pen from the nightstand, writes down something, and hands it to me. He continues, "These are the directions for it. That's where I'll be. You can contact me on this cell phone."

Just as the words leave his lips the motel room door bursts open and three masked gunmen run in. Without a word they motion and push Julie, Phillip and Joe into the bathroom. One of the guys holds a gun on me. I see one of the men awkwardly try to duct tape Winterfield's hands together. He tries pushing one of them away. The gunman hits him on the head with the butt of his gun, but this does nothing but draws some blood and daze Winterfield. It's enough, however, to allow them to drag him out of the room. I am alone with the last gunman who cocks his gun. He points it at me and turns and runs out of the room. I dart from the room in time to see a dark sedan screeching out of the parking lot. I slowly walk back to the room.

"Did you get a plate number?" Julie inquires.

"I thought we were in for it, Dad."

Phillip looks at me. We have been doing this together for some time now. He notices my wheels turning.

"Something is fishy. These are not the same guys who tried to kill us yesterday on the ocean. If they were, we'd be dead by now. This was pure amateur hour. I think we have another party after Winterfield," I surmise.

"What's our next move, Dad?"

"I think I'll call Gino. He's the most important character we have now. Then I think we head back to the island casino and visit Jennifer and bring her up to date. Phillip, you'll arrange a boat? And not one that flies. Maybe we could fish a little tomorrow. I always think better on the water. We'll check in with Caruso tomorrow too. He'll be back by then and maybe he'll have heard something."

"What do you want me to do?" Julie offers.

"Come with us?" I beg without begging.

"I'm afraid to check in with headquarters not knowing who's listening and how they may be connected. I'll call in for a couple of more days off. I have an uncle who was once chief of police down here. I just remembered him. I think he retired years ago, though he's an islander, as they say. Born here and will die here. He might be of some help. What do you say?" Julie asks.

"I'm not so sure about bringing anybody else into this case. I don't know what the case is anymore."

Phillip breaks in, "Jamaica, this is the homerun everybody dreams of. You're holding all the cards and, if you play them right, we'll have fishing money for a long time. We won't always have to use mine. You can control the outcome of this. You need to get Winterfield back in charge of his little domain down here. Jennifer and Martelli need to get a little piece to keep them quiet. You need to get the cash flow back to Gino, and you need to get Forester to use his contacts in Washington to stop their pushing Winterfield around."

"That sounds all well and good," I reply, "but I still think there's someone else involved here. Something doesn't fit. It feels like we have a square peg and we're trying to jam it through a round hole because it's the only opening we have left. I think we need to find the other opening."

"What's your goal: help Jennifer or go after the million dollars?" Julie asks.

"With some luck, we can do both; I don't trust Winterfield. The last time we spoke he tried to blow us all up if you remember?"

"I think we should call Jennifer and tell her we'll be there sometime tomorrow night, but we get there as early as possible," Julie plans.

"I think we call her from the boat just as we dock. It will give her less time to plan a surprise. Surprising people run in that crazy family." I retort.

CHAPTER TWENTY-SEVEN

ROLL THE DICE

We have a plan, not really a plan, more like an idea of what to do, but no idea what we'll do when we get there. Phillip will arrange transportation there and, of course, I'll wing it when we get there. It's been a heck of a day, to say the least. Phillip is going to get some sleep, and I suggest the same for Julie and Joe. Julie goes and checks in at the lobby for another room since she already checked out this morning to cover our little plan. I'm going to call Gino in the morning and bring him up to date. I have to admit, Joe is into this thing, and I seem to forget our bet. I dare not bring it up. The school season is one month away and he's still hanging on. It's a good sign.

Sleep comes quickly to my band of adventurers. We have a quiet night. Morning brings some fresh ideas to mind while I wait for the knock on the door signaling the start of our next venture out on the water.

Phillip arrives with coffee for four. Julie must have seen him coming and arrives at my room right after him. Joe and I are dressed to go. Phillip has arranged a boat to take us, but this time we'll drive. Boy, would I love to get my line wet just once while we're here.

Everyone seems tired. We all wait for the caffeine to hit before we start talking. We take the morning walk to the dock, pay the dockmaster and walk towards our rental.

The dock is humming with activity. Most of the boats are preparing for a day of cruising and fishing. What a life. Our boat is in slip twenty-four. It's not bad, a 1998 twenty-six-foot Grady White. We throw our things on board, start the batteries, put the bilge on, vent, and then check things out for any unexpected mechanical failures that seem to arise when you mix motors and saltwater, especially with a rented boat. Everything checks out for Phillip and me. Phillip starts the engine while Julie and Joe untie us from the dock.

Phillip steers us from the dock and into the harbor. Something has me turning around every few minutes, but I don't know why. I bet the second cup of coffee would have helped.

"You look nervous. What's wrong?" Julie inquires.

"I don't know; something on the dock caught my eye. These three guys were getting on a small Boston Whaler for a day of fishing," I puzzle.

"What's so different about that? We're in Florida, Dad."

"Most guys do not go fishing in Bally loafers and Joseph Abode shirts."

"Maybe they're here on business and that's all the clothes they have," suggests Phillip.

Phillip gets us in the channel and past the markers and opens up the boat. I turn around one last time; there are no trailers. We travel in silence for a while. I spot what I think is the forty-foot Tiara from the other day. It's heading full steam on the same coordinates as ours. He has come from a private dock further north than us. He breezes by us some sixty feet to the west of our path. He does not slow up. Casino travelers, headed for the same place, I surmise.

Looking at the charts I see we'll be at the dock in twenty minutes. So far, all is clear around us. The water is blue and calm. Sometimes crossing this channel between Florida and the Bahamas can be a killer. The constant hum of the engine keeps our minds relaxed. I motion to Phillip to slow it down a little to give us time to enjoy and think. Joe is seated below and Julie is stretched out on the seat next to Phillip, enjoying the scenery.

In the distance, I see the dock where we landed yesterday. The Tiara is docked port side, leaving us plenty of room to get in. We won't have to call Jennifer. She's waiting on the dock to greet guests from the Tiara.

"Slow up; let's see how she handles this."

Phillip idles the engine. We're only one hundred feet from the dock.

Jennifer greets the smartly dressed man with a warm hug. The guest looks right out of the boardroom, fifty-five, grey, trim and corporate, Tommy Bahama from head to toe. They walk to the waiting golf cart and take off onto the path leading into the woods.

"Let's go."

Phillip hits the throttle and quickly approaches the dock. He parks as if he's been driving this boat his whole life. Show off. Julie and Joe jump off; I throw them the lines and they tie us up. Phillip kills the engine. The captain from the Tiara comes out to check his lines, then walks to the cabana without giving us a second glimpse. So far so good: nobody has come out to greet us or shoot at us. Since this is a private island I figure someone knows we're here. I hear the sound of the golf cart coming back down the path. We walk up the dock, expecting to be stopped. Two golf carts appear, driven by Martelli and a casino worker, I presume. Martelli waves. Good sign.

"We were expecting you. Most guests are dressed a little nicer for a day of fun here, but then you look like rock stars. You know we had Michael Jordan here last week with a couple of friends, and they came dressed in fishing shorts."

"I don't think we'll be spending that type of money here," I offer.

"Get in. Jennifer's waiting," Martelli beckons.

Julie and I get in with Martelli while Joe and Phillip get in with the other driver. We follow the path through the trees. Things cool off right away because of the shade.

"How did you know we were coming?" I ask a stupid question.

"We have friends on the dock."

A clearing up ahead exposes a rich-looking, single-story Mediterranean-style building behind a circular driveway. Off to each side, angling toward the rear, are low villas that mimic the style of the main building. This place has big money written all over it. As we pull up to the entrance Jennifer walks out. Just at that moment my phone rings.

"How's everything going?" Caruso asks from the other end in New York.

"Fine," is all I reply. He knows I can't talk.

"I'll talk; you listen. Winterfield has been spotted in Las Vegas getting off a private jet this morning. He's not there for fun if you get my drift," Caruso teases.

"Very nice talking to you," I try to respond. Everyone is staring at me.

"I'm not done; it gets better. The boys down in the morgue are not so sure that Thomas Degan is really Thomas Degan. We can't get a match. It seems the hot tar decomposed his body rather quickly, and dental records cannot be found. Call me."

"Good news, Mr. Biltmore?" Jennifer inquires.

"I'm not sure yet. We can't seem to locate Winterfield. We spoke last night."

That's a bombshell about to go off. Martelli's and Jennifer's eyes fall out of their heads like those funny clown glasses with the eyes on springs.

"I suggest we go somewhere to talk," Martelli offers dryly.

Martelli leads all of us to one of the side villas which are located down a dirt path. He pulls a key from his pocket and opens the door. We all pile into the most luxurious hotel suite I have ever seen.

"Mr. Biltmore, you spoke with Winterfield last night and you did not call me? We had a deal. What am I paying you for?" Jennifer berates.

"We're here, right? We spoke for a minute, we were cut off and that was the last I heard from him. He's on the run and needs to talk with you to help him straighten this mess out," I lie through my teeth.

"You don't believe him, do you?" Jennifer asks incredulously.

"Why would he come to me? He's been trying to kill us for some time, and when people do that, we usually do not become friends. It's a policy of mine: Never become good friends with anyone who has tried to kill me three times or more without a good reason." I drone on. "It looks like you two have taken over his operations here. Was that your plan in the first place?"

Jennifer and Martelli exchange quick glances.

"I don't need an answer. Nevertheless, I bet you never thought it was going to be this easy, right? I don't know how much you know about this operation and your stepdad." Jennifer tries to cover up her shock. Oh boy, she didn't know I knew the family tree.

It's time for another voice to be heard from. I need to think of getting out of here and having her pay for a trip to Vegas for the four of us.

"Mrs. Degan, we need time to track him down," I say.

Phillip begins, "This is going to cost money and take a week or so. I suggest you two continue running this place, and we'll check in a day or two. Jamaica here will notify you where we go. You have to remember the men who were chasing us for the last couple of days want him badly. His connections go from Washington D.C. to these third-world countries, to the streets of New York, and finally into the boardrooms of the largest corporations in the world. This will get dangerous before it comes to an end." Phillip has completely scared the hell out of Martelli and Jennifer. Perfect. I couldn't have done it any better.

"Why don't I stay here to help out?" Julie offers.

I don't like this plan. "What a good idea." I introduce the women. "Jennifer, this is Julie Waters, FBI

Agent. Give her a job around here to blend in and she'll report to me any trouble that shows up. I have to ask: Winterfield has plenty of muscle. How did you two convince them not to stuff you in an oil drum and float you out into the Caribbean?"

Martelli's turn, "Jennifer can be very convincing. They think we're here to watch over things until he gets back from an overseas trip looking for another casino location and raising money. I think he knows we're here, but since we have not turned the place upside down he has made no attempt to wrestle this away from us now. As long as the money is still flowing he'll be okay with us."

"Mr. Biltmore, all this means that we don't have any funds for ourselves yet. I won't let this go on too long," Jennifer says without thinking.

"Don't do anything stupid just yet. Let this play out. I think you and Winterfield are in the same ballpark but sitting in different sections right now. We need to go." With that, Joe opens the door, and we all exit into the hot Caribbean sun. We walk in silence to the two golf carts still standing in front of the casino. Martelli calls over from the group of valets standing in front of the guard shack. He will drive us back to our boat. I pull Julie aside.

"You be careful. Call me at the slightest problem Watch for the gamblers who show up here. There has got to be a call center that takes all the gambling calls from around the world for these high-end bettors. There must be one hell of a computer set up too," I go on and on.

"Jamaica, I'll be fine. Where are you headed?"

"Vegas."

The gang is ready to go. Julie gives me a rub on the back. I pile into the golf cart with Joe. Phillip is in the other cart. Jennifer puts up her hand for us to wait. She runs inside. I hear the sound of another cart coming up the path; it's the three guys from the dock. Martelli sees me staring at them. He does not say anything until their greeter comes from the casino and takes them inside.

"Newly elected senators — Winterfield's reach is incredible," Martelli says admiringly.

"My advice is 'do not rock the boat.' I think the guys working for Winterfield are worse than the guys trying to kill him. That means the men here are very loyal to him and very ruthless. Keep that in mind."

Jennifer comes out with a folding leather portfolio that's stuffed with something. My heart races like a kid seeing a badly wrapped present under the tree on Christmas morning. Martelli takes off with a wave from Jennifer.

We head down the path toward the boat, one passenger lighter. I feel comfortable with Julie staying there, but I feel responsible for her at the same time. I bid Martelli goodbye, Phillip gets in the boat, starts the engines, and looks to me to untie us from the dock. Martelli takes care of the untying for us. Joe pushes off from the port side so we don't hit the piling.

We slowly head out into the clear, blue Caribbean waters. I look at Phillip, "I think that went quite well. You handled that like a pro. Can we fish for a little?"

"You tell me," Phillip shoots back.

"Dad, who called when we were inside the cabana? Your face was incredible; talk about a poker face."

Phillip sees me grabbing my fly rod and slows the boat down. He steers us out of the channel and into some flatter waters, not too far from the island from which we just came. I start setting up my rod. Joe takes my cue and gets his traveling spinning rod from his Brookstone case.

"Well?" Phillip begs.

"It was Caruso. Winterfield was kidnapped by someone who took him to Vegas on a private plane," I say nonchalantly.

I start some lazy roll cast toward a distant ripple.

"Jamaica, there's something you're not telling me," Phillip says puzzled.

"Caruso also said that the body supposedly belonging to my first client, Thomas Degan, might not be him."

That comment makes Joe's line go slack as he tries to reel it in, and Phillip's face practically falls off his head.

"Hey, I got something!"

I had never caught anything on a fly before in these waters. Judging by the action and the color, it's a nice, thirty-inch Dorado. It's dancing along the water, giving us a color show as the sun hits the wet body twirling in the air. My two helpers finally recover enough to help out. As I get the fish to the side of the boat, Phillip leans over and deftly removes the fly hook with one hand and holds the fish with the other. He pulls him up so we can take a quick picture before letting the little guy go back and enjoy the day. Here's an amazing thought: We get all bent out of shape when we head out for a day of fishing and get skunked, but we never think how annoyed the <u>fish</u> must be when we catch them. Oh well, that's what they're there for, right?

CHAPTER TWENTY-EIGHT

CRAPS

We enjoy the day on the water, even if it is only for an hour. I use the cell phone to make connecting flights for the three of us from Miami to Las Vegas. Las Vegas: Sin City, the town where anything goes and nothing seems real; the glitz, the all-nighters, the showgirls; the sound of coins hitting the specially designed metal trays at the bottom of the slot machines to catch the ear of all those nearby. Las Vegas: everything you'd want in an adult vacation – except fishing. How good could that be?

Our flight is set for four p.m. That will leave us enough time to get back to our motel, shower, pack, and get to the airport. Leaving Key West will be tough. I could see retiring here someday, but what would I do all day? Fish, swim, hang out with friends, explore the islands — how long could that last, twenty, thirty years? I'm sure I'd get bored after a while.

I always wanted to go to Vegas. Gino has told me about the good old days before the large corporations stepped in and bought up the place. It must have been exciting – the days of the mob, Frank Sinatra, and Dean Martin flying over from Los Angeles to do a show, spending the rest of the night in their tuxedos, gambling and carousing around the strip. In those days, the federal government and the SEC didn't regulate a thing. Everybody checked their conscience at the border and became James Bond with a martini in one hand, a blonde in the other, playing craps, wearing their white dinner jackets in the smoke-filled casinos. This is the town where they all came together, politicians, businessmen, mobsters, and entertainers. Their lives got intertwined and it took thirty years to break them apart. You would walk into The Flamingo Hotel and there, in the face of the public, you would have Frank Sinatra, the biggest entertainer of all time, having dinner with JFK and some mob boss from New York, and it never made the New York Post. Nobody blinked an eye. This place hummed with excitement.

Then the trouble hit after the Sixties. Everyone got a case of the stupids. The mob was not accepted as an organization that fit in with society. They were outcasts, and not very bright. They enjoyed the limelight and mixing with the elite of the business world. The growth rate of the casino business skyrocketed so that the stiffs in the boardroom could no longer be pushed around and controlled by politicians, and the mob became a huge monster to deal with. High-flying financiers like Michael Milken showed the greedy businessmen how to swallow up companies ten times larger than themselves with Monopoly money called junk bonds. The federal government started regulating casinos, and the bad guys could no longer do the famous money count —one for you, three for me. Then the suits invaded Vegas, and the complimentary meals and rooms for the big bettors went the way of the polyester leisure suit.

What never changed through all those years, though, were the big gamblers putting millions down on sporting events. Right after the mob fixed the famous Boston College basketball games in the Seventies, the local bookies, operating in the corner candy store, started working behind closed doors protected by passwords.

This is where Winterfield and his operation came into play. Times change, but people still love to bet, and some guys bet more than the gross national product of Paraguay in a single afternoon. Winterfield now accommodates them because the corporations who run Vegas will not. It's that simple. At least it was until we showed up.

The flight to Vegas is uneventful. Joe listens as long as he can to my history lesson before falling asleep. Phillip is asleep before the wheels leave the ground. Me, I don't like sleeping on planes; too many what-ifs going through my head. Joe has not spoken about college in days. This is a good sign.

I spot Lake Mead and Hoover Dam, which means we'll be landing soon. I can feel the neon lights pulsing through my veins as we start descending into McCarran Airport.

As we land and taxi to our gate, I stir the troops. Of course, there is a limo waiting for us, thanks to another of Phillip's connections. The guy is a marvel. The airport probably doesn't look any different than the airport in any other growing city, but I feel a difference. It feels glitzy and high class. When Steve Wynn owned The Mirage, Treasure Island, Golden Nugget, and the Bellagio, they should have let him rebuild this airport – we'd probably be riding through the streets of Venice in a gondola, going to pick up our bags.

Bags in hand, we head out into the heat. The difference between this heat and Key West heat is simple: In Key West, the ocean is ten minutes on either side of you; here it's a day away. The ride from the airport to our hotel, The Bellagio, is thirty minutes or so. Joe and Phillip are enjoying the scenery. It's been a while since Phillip was last here. His old friend is the senior vice president of finance at this new hotel. I have only seen pictures of it and heard that it cost one-point-six billion dollars to build. Somebody got ripped off I presume.

We turn in from the strip. Oh my God! There is a freaking lake in front of the place the size of Biscayne Bay. The three of us are standing in front of this hotel with our mouths hanging down as if Moses himself is walking down from the mountain with the Ten Commandments in his hand. The uniformed bellhop takes our three bags and places them on a cart that cost more than my car. We enter the cavernous marble lobby and the cool air is a relief from the oven outside. Instantly you hear the clanging of the slot machines paying off just enough money to keep people from realizing that they're footing the mortgage payments for this place.

Phillip heads for the concierge desk to announce our arrival to his friend. Joe and I are taken aback by the hustle and bustle of the activities going on in the lobby. The pretty girl behind the counter points to what I presume to be Phillip's friend strutting across the lobby from the casino floor. He is the spitting image of Andy Garcia's character in Ocean's Eleven. His suit fits him better than my underwear. They hug as if Phillip has just returned from the war. Phillip drags him over to Joe and me.

"Jamaica, Joe, I would like to introduce my brother-in-law, or should I say ex-brother-in-law, Steve Marshall. Steve this is the world-famous Jamaica Biltmore and his son Joe."

"Great to meet you. How was the flight?"

Before we can answer, he answers for us — a professional greeter.

"I used to hate the flights, but I have to do it once a month for meetings on Wall Street. We have to answer to so many people who backed this place, it's incredible. Come up to my office and we'll have lunch and talk. I'd rather not talk down here; too many civilians. Know what I mean?"

Steve whirls around and we break into a semi trot to keep up with him. I think he should lay off the caffeine.

We silently make our way to an elevator at the end of the long, gold lobby. Steve presses his left hand onto a black digital screen next to the elevator and the door opens. The elevator's wall panels have the creamiest marble I've ever seen. I rub my hand over it appreciatively.

To no one, in particular, Steve goes on, "Security is a wonderful thing. This is where the high rollers go. It's a shame we have to claim all this stuff. Some guy comes with a suitcase full of money, but you never know if he's a plant from the Nevada Gaming Commission or some lucky son-of-a-bitch who owns a cash business. I see you admiring the marble. When we were building, I spent time in Italy with the former owner — we're not allowed to say his name — hand-picking this stuff. Nice, huh?"

Just as he finishes, though I do not think he ever really stops talking, the door opens to what I would describe as a very private, upscale, decadent men's club.

Joe and Phillip walk around, checking out the surroundings. The place is set up as an entertainment Mecca: a teak bar with marble top in one corner, complete with a waitress who looks like a Sports Illustrated swimsuit model; two complete floor-to-ceiling window walls looking at the Vega strip; one wall with eight television monitors; a card table tucked in the corner, and a buffet table set up against the windows. There are five doors hidden in the beechwood-paneled walls leading to something I probably do not want to know about.

"Help yourselves, I'm sure you must be hungry. I could set up a line of credit if you want to try your luck downstairs, or you could get lucky up here if you want," he laughs at his own joke. Good thing, because he's getting annoying. I head for the bar and ask for a beer. Joe and Phillip prefer water right now. I open the teak humidor and a full box of Churchill Cohibas stares me in the face. I grab three and put them in my shirt pocket. I take the three drinks and head for the table.

Joe and Phillip are eyeing the lobster salad and shrimp when I join them. Steve is seated at the table, and the girl brings him a cup of coffee. I guess he needs to fuel the engine.

"What can I do for you, Mr. Biltmore?" A serious tone has crept into his voice.

I put my plate down and have a seat next to Steve. Joe and Phillip dive into their gold-rimmed plates. I would find these plates very tacky if we were in any other town; here, I would expect nothing else.

Chapter Twenty-Nine

Lesson Number One, Nothing Is As It Appears

It's time to take charge. I can see this turning into a duel, but I'm ready.

"We have this client."

"Winterfield, We all know him — kind of a thorn in our side."

"He disappeared from Key West yesterday."

"He's here, well not here but here, somewhere in town," Steve brags.

"He was taken by some corporate guys, not your usual leg breakers." This gets Joe and Phillip to lift their heads from their food. I'll explain how I know this throughout this verbal sparring.

"I agree with you. Even the corporate bad guys are not so bad."

"If it were the real 'bad guys who took him, he'd be dead," I guess.

"Right again. I'll give you guys a tour when we're done and you can see the operation we have here. It takes a lot of money to run a place like this."

I'd rather get a tour of Disneyland with that damn Mouse than listen to Steve drone on and on.

"That's obvious," I say, "but what does this have to do with Winterfield?" Acting dumb.

"See, Mr. Biltmore, there are a few casinos here in town that do not do as well as us. Some of those corporate guys are always looking for an angle to make a quick dollar. Winterfield is their conduit to that hidden cash. He still has a lot of pull here. He's been sending money to these guys for a long time, ever since they bankrolled him a couple of years ago."

"Let me guess: Since you can no longer skim cash off the top, some of these suits wanted some running-around money."

"Very good, Jamaica. How does ten million dollars a year sound?"

"Beats having a 7 –11."

Joe is done eating and needs to chime in. Good. "I still don't get why they brought him here."

"See Joe, since Winterfield has been playing both sides of the fence for so long, nobody wanted their gravy train to stop, Cash is king. One or two executives who run these large corporations couldn't care less about their salaries, bonus, and stock options when you're talking about ten million in unclaimed cash." I offer.

Phillip has enough information for a new book, which I'm sure we'll see soon enough, whenever this case is over. "Steve, do you have any idea where he's being held?"

"No, but with a phone call or two, I can find out. I have a room set aside for you three to wash up in. I guess you're flying out tonight?"

"Hopefully with Winterfield," I say.

"I'll help all I can."

With that Steve gets up and walks toward the elevator. His cell phone rings. He just listens and closes it when the conversation is over. He looks worried.

"There's a new guy in town from New York who is asking about Winterfield. You guys better be careful."

"Thanks for the help, Steve," I throw out.

"Anything for Phillip." With that, he gets into the elevator and disappears.

"Well. Who do we think our new visitor is, Dad?"

"This is a pure guess, but I have a funny feeling that Thomas Degan is among the living present."

Even Phillip is stunned at that one. "Come on, do you think he's behind all of this?"

"It would make sense. I think he's trying to stop us and get Winterfield back to New York."

"One thing I don't get: Who brought Winterfield here?" Phillip asks.

"Some corporate guy who's worried about his ten million dollars, like your buddy said," I guess.

"What's our next step, Dad?"

"Let's get cleaned up and see if your friend can lead us to Winterfield. We need to get him back, at least for Gino's sake. How about a walk on the strip to think about this?"

"Dad, it's a hundred and ten degrees outside. Let's go into the air-conditioned casino; I have to see one of these places."

Sternly, I tell him, "Son, you're only eighteen. You must be twenty-one to get in, It's the law." I look over at Phillip who can't believe I just said that. Joe looks rejected.

"All right, just this once." I push the button for the elevator and Joe walks in first as Phillip pulls me aside.

"Are you kidding?"

"I wasn't going to stop him."

We ride in silence to the lobby to face throngs of tourists arriving to rid themselves of their money. I have to admit, a weekend here with the guys would be a blast, if only they had fishing. Oh well. We exit the elevator banks and two large suits come up to us and stand alongside me. They do not shop in the same suit place as Steve Marshall. Phillip and Joe are nudged behind us.

Quietly the one to my right says, "Mr. Biltmore, I think you should come with us, alone."

Not to alarm the crowd and get us thrown out of the hotel, I turn to Phillip and Joe, "Tell Steve I'll accept his hospitality for that room later. I'm going to take a ride with these nice fellows in their bad suits, and I'll be back with Winterfield."

My cockiness gets me a poke in the ribs with what I take to be a snub-nose .38 revolver. The pace has picked up as we leave the lobby to enter the scorching sunlight. Between Joe, Phillip, and myself it would be no problem getting rid of these two accountants, but I need to find Winterfield before Degan does.

We make it past the taxi stand, and a white van comes screaming up to us. The sliding side door flies open to reveal two more thugs, who at least look the part. The big, hairy guy is holding a sawed-off shotgun. Talk about your contrasting styles. He addresses the two suits. "We advise you to leave Mr. Biltmore right here." The grip on my arms goes slack, I'm sure their knees have weakened too, and I don't want to look down on the ground for the puddle.

"Let him go and head back to Mr. Banks. Tell him our mutual friend does not appreciate you dragging Mr. Biltmore all the way out here. Tell Mr. Banks we would like to see Mr. Winterfield back here at the Bellagio this evening. Go." With that, the suits scatter like leaves in a hurricane.

"Thanks, guys."

"Uncle Gino says hello. He appreciates you coming all the way here. Have a nice flight back with Winterfield, and Gino will meet you back in New York. He'll contact you there."

The door slides shut and the van drives away slowly. Phillip and Joe, who are frozen near the revolving door, come running over.

"What the hell was that all about, Dad?"

"Gino has friends all over. He knew who had Winterfield, and he ordered the two suits to bring him back to us in one hour. Let's go gamble; I feel lucky."

We march back into the hotel. Steve is there to greet us.

"Here are your room keys. I've arranged for fresh clothes to be in your room. How about dinner around seven? We'll meet in the casino by the private baccarat tables. We'll have a good time." He hands Phillip the keys to a suite on the tenth floor.

We stroll past the lines of people waiting impatiently to check in and over to the elevator bank. We have some extra cash from Jennifer, so we can have some fun.

From the tenth floor, even the views from the corridor are incredible. Phillip opens the door to a suite the size of a hockey rink.

"Guys I'm going to lie down for twenty minutes; wake me then," I leave my two partners, make my way into the bedroom, and fall onto the cool sheets. I drift off.

That was the quickest nap I ever had. I hear Joe and Phillip from the other room, "We'll meet you in the casino; there are clothes in the closet." With that, the large door slams shut.

I put the light on and see a package of clothes, from underwear and socks to newly polished shoes. In the closet are a white dinner jacket, black tuxedo pants, a white shirt, and a black bow tie. This guy might be okay after all. I shower quickly and get dressed; the clothes fit perfectly. He even put the cigars I pilfered from our first meeting into the pocket of the jacket. I can't help but stare at myself in the mirror. The pocket of the jacket feels heavy. I put my hand in and pull out twenty-one hundred-dollar chips. This guy is okay. Cigar in hand, I strut down the corridor, past some twenty-dollar-a-day gambling tourists. I feel like a king. Riding down in the elevator, I have to look at myself in the reflection of the gold-trimmed elevator door. In the lobby, I head for the casino floor, following the overhead signs toward the baccarat tables. The tables are blocked off from the rest of the casino floor by a gold and back railing and two nice-looking fellows wearing uniforms and earpieces to listen to a security guard watching from above.

"Good evening, Mr. Biltmore. We have a table for you waiting," He turns and leads me to a table in the corner. There's a small crowd watching two distinguished gentlemen and one fine-looking lady at play.

"Is this seat taken?" I say to no one in particular as I sit. A long-legged cocktail waitress comes to the table. "I'll have a rum martini."

One of the gentlemen stares at me. "This is a very friendly game, sir."

"That's all the better with me. I'm here for the laughs." This defuses the situation. The young lady to my right stares at me, "You are?"

Here I go, "Biltmore, Jamaica Biltmore." Maybe this really does beat fishing.

I feel a tug on my leg; what the hell.

"Dad, it's time to get up. It's ten minutes to seven. Phillip and I already showered. There are some clean clothes on the other bed. They're not great, but they fit."

I try to shake the cobwebs from my head, God, that was some dream.

I shower again, this time for real. I dress quickly and put on my pants with the Bellagio golf shirt. I look at my socks standing up in the corner, waiting for me to jump into them, then over at the new lime green Bellagio complimentary socks, and decide no socks would be better. I see my three confiscated cigars on the dresser. I grab one and head down for dinner. Boy, I thought that dream was real! I catch up with Joe and Phillip, having a ball at the slot machines and flirting with a waitress. Across the casino floor, I see Steve traveling faster than a speeding bullet with two young men in tow kicking up dust, not unlike Pig Pen from 'Charlie Brown.' He arrives with a full head of steam, gathering his minions, and were off we go to dinner.

"You look good in our golf shirts."

I guess I should thank him, but he probably won't hear. "Where are we going?" I inquire.

"You like steak? Good. I have a table all ready to go for us. If your Winterfield character shows up, we'll be called.

We burst through the doors of the steak house like John Wayne arriving from a long ride on the prairie.

We're ushered to a table in the back. Waiters and waitresses swarm around us. Food seems to arrive the minute we sit down.

"I took the liberty of pre-ordering for us. This is how we treat our high-rollers. We find out what they like ahead of time and keep it in our computer system so, when the guy comes in, we bounce. We know his brand of scotch, what type and year of wine he likes, and the country where he prefers his cigars from. We know if the lady with him is his wife or girlfriend and, best of all, we know how much he can lose before he blows his cool."

"It sure beats the mint on the pillow at night." I try for a laugh. Steaks are thrown down in front of us along with an assortment of vegetables, salads, and potatoes. Wine is poured into our wafer-thin Riedel stemware.

"There are so many casinos on one street for this guy to lose his money in, we've got to have an edge and give him the little extra incentive to come to our place."

"Then why put the pressure on the big sports bettors and drive them out of town?"

"Good question, Mr. Biltmore. I thought they were good for business, but the stockholders did not agree. Big bettors became associated with shady characters and fixed games and kids going to jail. What scared some of the big corporations was that some of these guys had a winning record. I look at it like this: If one guy takes you for a million a week, it doesn't matter. The cash that goes through here on a good night is mind-boggling. We need all the gamblers we can get. The Bahamas, Connecticut they have one or two casinos for competition. They also have the whole east coast to pull from. Every one of those high-end sports bettors has many friends who think they gamble as well as he does, but they don't, which means they lose a lot. That's why I like the big-time sports bettors."

Joe has finished his meal and looks bored. "Is there a time when these guys just bet smaller amounts and stay here in Vegas for the thrill of the place?"

"That's very good, kid. That's exactly what's happening. Some guys just can't get enough of this place. They curb their appetite, placing smaller bets. My bosses find that acceptable, and I get to keep the guys in town. High rollers bring in other high rollers. You do not build these massive places unless you win most of the time, no matter the size of the bet. The guys who built and own these places become the billionaires, not the gamblers or the wise guys used to run them."

That statement hits the table like a ton of bricks falling off the back of a truck. I think about all the people involved in this long and winding case, and the only one with real money, I mean <u>real</u> money, is probably Winterfield, and he knows it. I have to admit, looking across at Phillip, he does well whenever he writes a best-seller, but there you need talent. With Winterfield, it's who you know, timing, and big balls.

The hostess comes up to Steve and whispers into his ear.

"Winterfield is here. Security has him."

I get up and reach for Steve's hand to shake it. "This has been great. Your hospitality is wonderful. Joe, come with me. Phillip, we'll catch up later before we catch the redeye home. Thanks again, Steve."

"Any time. You have to come back soon for the fun of it. The hostess here will lead you to our security room. I'll let them know you're coming."

JAMAICA BILTMORE; CASH GUNS & FLY RODS

With that, Joe and I leave the table and follow the hostess out. We're handed over to a roving security guard who leads us away from the casino floor and into a back corridor. At every door, the guard either enters a code, uses a passkey, or presses his hand against a black digital screen for identification. We reach our destination: security central. I doubt if the New York City Police Department has a computer set up as elaborate as this. There's not a place in the casino that cannot be seen from here. I'm afraid to ask if they can see into the guest rooms. Seated in the corner, having a cold beer, is Winterfield.

"Nice to you see you again, Mr. Biltmore. I see by the look on your face you're not so surprised to see me."

"When you were taken from Key West, I did suspect you'd be in trouble. The guys who took you were not the thugs we've encountered on this journey. What would you say if I told you that your stepson is alive?"

Winterfield stands up and slowly walks over to me. "How can this be? You said he was killed right in front of your eyes."

"I think I was set up. The guy who came to see me was sent by your stepson and probably didn't know he was going to be killed. He probably thought he was fronting for Thomas to keep him safe. Good employees will do that for some people."

"I can't believe it. Why?"

"Dad, if you might let me."

I look at Joe, not hiding my surprise.

"See, Mr. Winterfield, Thomas did not care about the construction business at all, though he and his partner, Robert Martelli, who also is alive, wanted a piece of your gambling business. Your stepdaughter talked Martelli into trying to get you out of the picture, and Thomas wanted everyone out of the picture."

"That's very good, son."

"What's our next step to avoid Thomas trying to kill us all? Greed is a great motivational tool." Joe says.

"I think it will help when we get you back to your island and sort things out with Martelli and Jennifer; I'll help sort things out with Gino. We need to have Thomas thinking we're going back to New York and get him to meet Captain Caruso of the New York City Police Department. We need to have two planes leaving from McCarran Airport with the ruse that we are on the one leaving for New York, so Thomas can follow. I'm sure he's convinced some people here in town that you've turned bad; that's why you were brought here. Your investors just want you safe and sending the cash back to them."

"That's very good, gentlemen. I'm glad I agreed to pay you all that money. I always like to keep my people motivated. When do we leave?"

"Within the hour; stay here. The boss man will come to get you. It might get a little uncomfortable until we're on our way, but we need to be safe."

Joe and I walk out of the security room. I see Phillip walking towards us with Steve.

"What's up, Jamaica?"

"Phillip, I want to get him back to New York right away. Steve, we need a place to talk without ears."

Steve has a puzzled look on his face. Then he motions us to follow. We take the elevator down to the lower-level gym. Through the glass doors and past the weight machines we enter the deserted men's locker room. Steve motions the attendant over.

"These men are conducting a safety test here. It's off-limits to guests for ten minutes."

The attendant doesn't answer, just nods and follows directions. We walk in and Steve turns on the showers. "As far as I know, we have yet to put any listening devices in here, and cameras get too foggy."

"Good. We need to get Winterfield out of the building, to the airport, and onto a plane. My thinking is a laundry truck and a large basket for him to hide in. You, make a phone call and get the word out on the street that you saw us making plans for getting Winterfield to New York. We need somebody to act as a decoy. Joe and I will get Winterfield out of here and to the plane leaving for Miami and down to his private island. I'll call Gino and give him a heads-up regarding the arrival of Thomas Degan. I want to be out of here in one hour. Steve, I need you to make the flight arrangements and the phone call. Can you also have housekeeping get us a huge laundry basket to the security room?"

"I got it all," Steve says with excitement. He pulls away from the shower and is instantly on his cell phone. Within minutes his part is done.

"Let me guess, I'm going to play Winterfield?" Phillip asks.

"You got it. We need to get Winterfield's clothes, a hat, and a lot of security guards to shield him from outside eyes."

We look at each other. "Let's go."

Back in the security room, Winterfield is bent over one of the monitors, inquisitive as a competitor might be. The laundry basket arrives and Winterfield eyes it.

"You guys have to be kidding. I'm not worried about Thomas."

"You might not be, but I'm not so sure he's alone. I have not gotten to Gino yet and, if Thomas somehow reached Gino and promised to bring you back or even get rid of you, then we need to be very careful. I need you and Phillip here to change clothes."

Phillip and Winterfield go into a side room and swap clothes. The phalanx of the security guard arrives. Phillip takes the hat off one of the guards, bows his head, and makes his exit. We watch on the monitors as he walks down the back corridor and into the very crowded lobby. The cameras have a full view of the lobby. We spot someone in the right corner acting like a tourist reading a brochure. Steve has the security guard who's working the monitor switch camera one to follow this suspect. We watch Phillip and his escorts leave the hotel and push their way through the arriving crowd and into a waiting smoked glassed limo van. Our suspect has taken the bait and hails a cab that, we surmise, will follow the van.

It's time for us to leave. I shake Steve's hand and promise to call when we get to our destination. Winterfield gets into the laundry basket, we hide his body with clean white sheets, and proceed out the security doors where I come to a dead stop.

"What's wrong, Dad?"

"We have to go out the lobby while the laundry basket goes out the.."

Steve slaps his hands together, "the loading dock."

Steve goes back into the security area and calls for somebody from housekeeping to come down.

"She'll take it through the loading dock area while we go through the lobby so I can wish you a good flight to New York."

Within a minute a woman arrives and takes over our mission. We stay back as the woman, under Steve's direction, pushes the cart into the back service corridor and out onto the loading dock.

Steve, Joe, and I walk through the lobby as planned. We get to the checkout line.

"Don't worry, we've taken care of everything, Mr. Biltmore. Your bags have been sent to the airport. Have a nice flight to New York. Please come back. I'll send Phillip back in a couple of days." Steve laughs at his own joke, slaps me on the back, and shakes Joe's hand.

We're off. We exit the lobby and say goodbye to Las Vegas for now. A limo is waiting and we head toward the airport. On the ride to the airport, the driver is in constant contact with other security personnel regarding the whereabouts of the suspect we think is Thomas Degan or at least a cohort. Everything seems to be going as planned. The driver says that Winterfield is on the plane to Miami and Phillip is on the plane to New York. The suspect has boarded the plane also.

Joe and I thank the driver, and I remind him to thank Steve for his help as he hands us our tickets. I'm very impressed with the power of these casino bosses in this town. We board the plane for Miami.

Joe and I take our seats in first class, right next to Winterfield, who is already seated and facing the window, trying to stay out of view of the boarding passengers. The plane's door closes. I let out a sigh of relief.

"Nice work, Mr. Biltmore."

With that, the restroom door opens and a gentleman walks out and over to us. He leans over the seats.

"Hello, Dad."

Winterfield looks at me. I shrug.

CHAPTER THIRTY

RED EYE

Damn, I thought I had this planned so well. I wonder if good old Steve had anything to do with this. Well, nothing can happen while we're up here. Maybe we can straighten this whole mess out by the time we reach Miami? Joe looks over at me as if to say, there goes the million dollars. I'm sure he's scanning college catalogs in his brain. I can't blame him if he is.

"So, Mr. Degan, that was a nice little trick you pulled in New York. I might not be a legal whiz, but I think there are a lot of people who frown on having somebody take your place and only to be killed."

Quietly, he says, "Very good, Mr. Biltmore, but I have proof that the person I hired to go see you were not killed by me but by my ex-partner."

"Any time you want to chime in here, Winterfield, it might shed some light on the situation," I suggest.

Winterfield looks around and I know what he's thinking: There are too many people here to discuss this. "What do you want with me, Thomas?"

"What I always wanted, to be part of your development deals. I would have been happy with that. Granted, Jennifer and Robert had other ideas when it came to what side-business you were involved in. I grew up admiring you and your business sense, but when I married Jennifer, it all came crashing down."

"If you had listened to me and not married her, things would have been different. She was the worst kind of gold digger," he rasps, wanting to be understood but trying to keep his tone hushed. "Also, that partner of yours is no bargain either. First, he started all those complaints about your construction company getting pushed around by my company, then he stuck his nose into areas where he should not have. You should have reined him in. I warned you. Some people I deal with did not want their little empires stepped on by your partner. They all had a life to protect, and some stupid businessman was not going to get in their way."

"I assume you're talking about those crazy guys in the building department?" I ask.

"Exactly. Developing was a small part of my business, as you've come to know, Mr. Biltmore, but it's something I built, and it's all mine. Granted, the money is better in this other venture, but in developing, I didn't have to split it with anyone."

I see Joe getting bored. I think I've lost him. "Okay, fellows, what's our next step? I have Gino to worry about, some corporate guys trying to straighten you out, and lastly Jennifer and Martelli to stop from killing you both — I think."

"Mr. Biltmore, I need to have a private conversation with Thomas about his future. I can straighten out any legal issues he might have with the dead guy from New York. I appreciate your efforts with Gino, and your friends in Las Vegas can help with the corporate guys. All everyone wants is their money. I think we can right everything, but some people might get burned over this. I'm willing to take that chance if the conversation goes well with Thomas, here."

He's willing to take that chance; what a big guy. He is smooth. He just bought himself another partner in his stepson, a small price for keeping somebody in his corner. He now has me and Thomas against Jennifer and Martelli: not bad maneuvering at thirty thousand feet. It's amazing what you can get done in first-class; it's a shame we can't get peanuts anymore.

I excuse myself and nod toward two empty seats in the rear of first-class for Joe and me. We make our way back to the seats. I decide to defuse the situation with the stewardess who is coming toward us.

"We just need to have a business conversation. I promise to return to my seat as soon as I can." Joe and I sit in the big leather chairs.

"I don't know, Dad. Remember, back on the navy base, how worried Uncle Bill was about this guy? I mean, he's fooled everyone from the CIA and FBI to naval intelligence just to get what he wants. What makes you believe him now?"

A good question. "I think he's realized that Thomas has some of his ruthlessness, and he's not to be messed with. Something, though, strikes me as very odd. All this can fall into place with a couple of conversations and agreements between parties? It's too easy. He's practically throwing money at us for talking with Gino and getting Gino to stay off his back."

"Wouldn't you pay to have Gino stay away from you?"

"Yes, I would, but he doesn't have to. All he has to do is make a payment, and Gino will slip under the covers again. Gino just wants money. I'm sure he has to spread it around too, but Winterfield can call him and take care of it."

"But Dad, Winterfield is on the run from Thomas and the Vegas guys, and Gino wants him found and returned to protect his investment."

"I don't think Thomas is acting alone. There's somebody bigger out there behind him. Something is missing or, should I say, someone, is missing from the equation."

I see Winterfield motioning us to come back. This should be good. I can't wait for the bull story that comes from this meeting. I can't believe Thomas is just rolling over after one conversation in first class.

Joe and I walk back toward our seats. I sit next to Winterfield; Joe sits next to Thomas.

"Mr. Biltmore, we have come to an understanding."

No shit.

"Thomas is going to work for me down here. If I can straighten out Jennifer and Martelli, we'll have a working relationship. I can use all the family I can get. I need to trust people down here while I head back to New York and wrap up some important business deals regarding our next casino."

I could throw up. Is he kidding or what? I excuse myself and head back to the rear of the plane. I open the curtain that separates first class from the other people on the plane. Talk about a capitalistic symbol — a curtain separating seats with a cost differential of two thousand dollars per seat. The seats, even where these peons are sitting, all have phones attached. Granted this call will cost more than the rent on my bar, but I need to talk with a reasonable person: Caruso.

I tell the stewardess I need to make an important phone call in private, and she steers me to the rear of the plane where there is an empty row of seats. I take out my credit card and swipe it through the phone. As instructed, I dial Caruso's cell phone and he picks up in one ring.

"Guess who's on the plane with me? Of course Winterfield. Thomas Degan found out about my little diversion and slipped on this plane. Yes, that Thomas Degan. Well, the boys down in the morgue must be mistaken because right now he's sitting in my seat, talking with Winterfield. I don't think we need to worry about this part anymore. I need to get Winterfield back to his casino and smooth things over with Gino. Okay, I'll let you talk. " I listen intently.

Joe finds me in the back of the plane and leans into the seat where I'm responding to Caruso.

"Why didn't you tell me? This is terrible. Is the press making a big thing about it? I didn't think so; nobody knew him. (I listen.) No, I never met his son, a lawyer of some type. (I listen.) Who? (Listening some more...) No shit? OK, I'll call from Miami." I reach into my pocket and pull out Julie's card with her phone number on it.

"Do me a favor: Call Julie at 555-555-1342 and tell her to meet us in Miami. Tell Phillip to check in at the bar and then get his ass back down here. I'm going to need all the official help I can get." I hang up the phone.

"What was that all about?"

"The police have not figured out if Thomas is dead or alive."

"Dad, he's sitting right there."

"I know that you know that, and Thomas knows that, but the New York City Police department doesn't know that. This stuff happens all the time. Maybe he's a twin-like those girls on the football beer commercials."

"Right, Dad. What else did he say? Your face is showing all kinds of strain like you couldn't make up a story fast enough."

"Sit down, Joe."

Joe squeezes past me into the empty seat. Boy, first class is nice, especially when somebody else is paying for it. I need to tell him about Caruso's news, then ask about this college stuff.

"Dad, would you ever consider moving away from New York?"

Where did this come from? "Why? Where?"

"You love fishing so much, does it really matter where we live?"

I have to keep an open mind. This is something I've never had over the years, but I'm willing to give it a shot. "What do you have in mind?"

"When I was lying around the motel in Key West, I saw a lot of commercials for a college in Fort Lauderdale. It looked great. I mean, I couldn't get in now because it's too late for the fall, but in the winter, when you get all crabby because of the weather, it would be a neat place to live and, if we moved down here, the cost would not be so bad considering we'd be a resident of the state and you could fish and find missing old people down here.

I'm sure they're missing all the time, probably because they can't remember their way home, but I'm sure they have money to pay you and—"

"Stop. You're giving me a headache. I get your point; take a breath." I need to think. This is one of those situations that I am not familiar with. There's a word that slips my mind that fits this type of thinking and warrants a response, but I can't think of it.

"You know, Dad, it would be a compromise."

Gong, gong, gong. I knew it was out there. That's an awful big word for an old guy like me. I don't know if I'm capable of such a thing. My ex-wife didn't think so.

"What else did Caruso say?"

"Gino died of a heart attack in the middle of the night. The press is not even running the story about him. He was under their radar the whole time. His son claimed the body."

"His son, the lawyer?"

"Yes, nice listening. The kicker is, the son is working as an aid to Senator Johnson from New York. Senator Johnson is no longer the senator from New York.."

"Isn't he some big-shot in Washington?"

"Exactly. He's now head of the CIA."

"That's big. What's our next step, Dad? Do we just get him back to his casino, straighten out Jennifer and Martelli and head home?"

"It seems that simple, doesn't it? I think there's still a missing link. I know I've said that before, but I think someone else is trying to muscle Winterfield out."

"Do you think Gino's son and the head of CIA are involved?"

"There's definitely a connection of some sort. Let's head back to our seats and chat with Winterfield and see what he knows about this connection."

As we reach the steel curtain of first-class the stewardess stops us. She does not recognize us. I point through the curtain at our seats, which are now occupied by Winterfield and Thomas. I inform the first-class cop that our tickets are in the bag on the floor. Winterfield hears the commotion and waves us over. Somehow this convinces the guard of the leather seats that we belong up here with the rest of the overpaying customers.

We walk, heads held high, back to our oversized seats.

"Are you two finished?" I inquire.

"I think we have come to an understanding," Winterfield proclaims.

"How well do you know Senator Johnson?"

God, he doesn't even blink. To him, it probably is just another investor in the grand scheme of things. To me, it's a guy who can take out a foreign leader at the drop of a phone call or empty a bank of all its money in the name of democracy.

"He's part of that Washington Fund, as I like to call it. Why do you ask?" Think fast; do not spill about Gino yet; think fast.

"My friend, Captain Caruso said Johnson just resigned from the CIA yesterday. I took a shot that you would know him."

Joe has a deadpan look on his face. He's got it.

"I know a lot of people, Mr. Biltmore. You know my past. These guys come and go, but the only constant is me. I'm sure we'll see Senator Johnson on my island casino by the time we get down there."

Oh boy, I didn't think of that. Winterfield will hear about Gino in a couple of hours. My influence will no longer be needed, and neither will he need to pay me. If Jennifer and Martelli still feel threatened by Thomas here, then my services might still be warranted. I must remember: I'm still a client of both Jennifer and Winterfield.

We have about one hour before we land. Winterfield has zoned out and is facing out the window, looking at nothing. Thomas has settled into his chair, leafing through a magazine. Joe has his head against the other window, which means he'll be asleep in ten minutes, leaving me to figure out a way out of this mess.

Compromise. What a strange thought. Would I like to live in Florida? Leaving the bar and our friends would be tough. I have gotten used to New York. It's a great city. Why did they build it there? Maybe they should have built-in Florida; the greatest city in the world, and look where it is!

I just don't know. I'll need to run this past Phillip. He's always the voice of reason, Caruso too. Sometimes when my mind is jumbled, like now, I seem to find an answer to my problems. I find myself drifting off to sleep. That won't work. I'm a tough PI from New York City; if I can't fight sleep, I'm not worth my salt. We'll be in Miami in forty-five minutes and my phony-baloney job will be at an end. If that does not motivate me, nothing will. I need a miracle.

"Dad, wake up. We're here."

Joe is tugging at me again. Winterfield and Thomas are already off the plane. I jump up, grab my carry-on, and exit the plane. At the end of the ramp, they're waiting for us. The Florida heat seeps through the walls.

"We'll need to get a taxi to Caulks Airlines and then a seaplane to the island. I'll call ahead for reservations," Winterfield says.

We start walking toward the bank of payphones when the headlines from the newsstand hits me like a hockey puck off of Bobby Hull's stick. (What can I tell you, I don't know any new players?) I head over to buy the paper; Winterfield is on phone already and Thomas and Joe are making small talk. My guardian angel has intervened yet again. I gape at the story in the New York Times, above the fold, in the right column, most important story of the day: 'Senator Johnson Subpoenaed.'

I read the story as quickly as possible. This job has prepared me for reading upside down, in Spanish, and from somebody's desktop while the secretary is gone to fetch me a cup of coffee. Johnson is one step away from jail for hiding his involvement in a gambling operation in Las Vegas. No mention of Winterfield or the islands. Good.

I bring the paper to Winterfield and show him the headlines while he's on the phone. He takes the paper and scans the article much as I did. He hangs up the phone.

"I guess we won't be seeing the senator down island anytime soon."

God, he's cold.

"We have our reservations set. The plane departs when we get there."

Winterfield walks away from us and toward the taxi stand. We all follow like little puppies. That's pretty impressive: The plane leaves when we get there, not at a certain time.

I need to call Forester and get his take on things. I let the party get out of earshot.

Then I quickly call Phillip at the bar. I need him to get down here. I dial quickly, screwing up the number twice. He already has plans for coming down this afternoon. Caruso called him. I need him to get Captain Ryan again. In my experience, when politicians start getting in trouble, the whole pyramid starts collapsing. I hang up the phone and head for the waiting taxi.

Chapter Thirty-One

Once Around The Mulberry Bush

I can feel cases coming to an end before they terminate. I thought this one was coming to an end a few times. This case is starting to feel like a bad western where all the good and bad guys are arriving in Dodge at the same time for one showdown. I look through the revolving door at Joe, Winterfield, and Thomas waiting for me in the cab. Within a couple of hours, we'll all be on Winterfield's private island. I'm sure he's got a private army of security guards that we'll have to deal with if things get out of hand. I watch Joe make small talk as I enter the cab. The voices around me do not penetrate my brain. My mind feels like a hot Texas night with tumbleweed rolling around inside. I cannot make heads or tails of a thought. I'm starting to panic. I feel sweaty and lightheaded. I reach for the window and push the down button. The hot air feels good as we make our way onto the highway toward Watson Island for Chalks Airline Terminal. Whew, I almost lost my cool there. The voices are starting to make sense.

"Dad, Mr. Winterfield here says he knows the President of Miami University. He'll get me in whenever I want."

"That's great, Joe." No, it's not. I thought I had him on this case. I mean if I was not a private eye, I'd <u>want</u> to be one after this case. It's got everything you'd ever want: shootings, falling elevators, hot tar, dead people coming alive, and a beautiful FBI agent. What a great life. As these petty thoughts are rattling around in my head, our path to the seaplane terminal is blocked by two black BMW 745s with dark-tinted windows.

"Dad?"

"I see them, Joe. Winterfield, down, you too, Joe." I look at Thomas.

"Don't look at me."

"Well, at least they didn't start shooting yet."

With that, a large gorilla in an undersized Hawaiian shirt gets out of the driver's side of one of the BMWs and pulls out a .357 magnum from his waistband, and shoots the tires of our cab. Well not exactly, it takes all of his six bullets to hit two of the tires. The cab driver is pissed. He's yelling at the guy through the windshield in some foreign language. At least I know the shooter is out of bullets for now. Who knows about the rest of the riders in the car? I decide to do something stupid: get out of the car.

As I open my door, the door to the other BMW opens, and a matching gorilla gets out of the driver's side. It's the Olsen twins on steroids.

"I know you two." They are the same two slabs of meat from the bar.

"Mr. Biltmore, we don't want to hurt you or your son; we want Winterfield."

God, I love the warm air. I can think. I wish I could be sure whether they are alone in those cars. I know Thing One is out of bullets and Thing Two has a full gun, though I can't see it at this time. I walk over to the one with the gun in hiding. I need to check out the cars.

"I've got no problem turning Winterfield over to you guys, but how do I know that, once I do, your passengers will not open fire at Joe and me?" If they fall for this, I'll wet myself with laughter.

"Mr. Biltmore, our boss is not with us; we're alone. We just want Winterfield."

When I used to take Joe to school, I was always amazed when some parents did not understand why their son or daughter was doing so poorly in school. sometimes they overlooked the obvious — the kid was plain dumb. Case in point – Thing One and Thing Two.

I make my way closer to Thing Two to get a look at his hidden gun. I catch a glimpse of an awkward bulge protruding from his side. From my new angle, I can see the car is empty, just as he said.

"Where are you taking him?"

"That's none of your concern. I want him out of the car now," Thing One exclaims.

The noise of a car door slamming catches our attention. The irate cab driver has gotten out of the car, ranting, and raving. He's swinging a sawed-off baseball bat and charging at Thing One who points his empty gun at him. I lunge for the buried gun on Thing Two, who falls back against the car door. The crazy-ass driver has El Kabonged Thing One with the bat. I have the gun pointed at Thing Two. Winterfield, Thomas, and Joe exit the cab.

"That was very good, Dad."

I decide to play tough guy. I point the gun at Thing Two. "Who hired you guys?"

He breaks quicker than a water glass under a cement truck.

"All I know is I got a call on my cell phone from someone named Thomas Degan. I swear. We get paid by cash in a safe deposit box in New York."

This guy is going to go on and on. I'll find out his third-grade teacher before long. We all look at Thomas.

Sheepishly, he admits, "I needed some muscle back in New York. They work for a friend who owns a bar downtown. I needed to shut Jennifer up. I never knew she had the same plan as I did. We both wanted a piece of the pie from dear old stepdad."

Winterfield is silent.

"Dad, why don't we use these guys to help us? We could use all the help we can get."

I don't know. These guys were pushovers. I need to make a phone call. Thing One is waking up.

"Winterfield, you pay the cab driver for his troubles. Let's get to the plane. Thomas, you help with your two henchmen. I need to make a phone call."

The terminal to Caulks Airline is a couple of hundred feet away. Winterfield pays the driver in cash with a nice tip. We head to the terminal, Thing One is holding his head. Anybody looking at us would think we just came from forty days in the desert. I grab my bag from the cab. Winterfield does the same and reaches inside his to give me his cell phone. I let the walking dead get ahead of me as I dial Caruso.

"Yes, it's me. We're fine. I need you to get all the information you can regarding Robert Martelli. I think I found the missing link to this case. Ten-to-one he's got a background to match Winterfield. I'm thinking CIA, large corporate guy, or worse. I'll call back when we hit the island. Yes, we're okay. Thanks."

As I close the phone it rings. I quickly flip it open and look toward Winterfield to see if he heard it. He did not. "Yeah."

The other voice tells me that everything is all set as planned and hangs up. It's time to fly. I run to catch up with the gang. Winterfield is inside the terminal block building. This is where the legendary Chalk Airline got started. It would be cool, but I have other things on my mind.

Thomas and the two numbskulls are standing by the hangar, looking at the seaplane. Joe is waiting for me outside the building. I can see Winterfield talking very animatedly with the pilot and the girl behind the counter. This is his territory.

"What do you think, Dad?"

"It's all coming together. Julie is waiting for us, Phillip is on his way down. I hope he's contacted Captain Jim; Caruso has called Forester for backup. I think we have all our bases covered."

"What are you expecting?"

"I don't know. I think Martelli is the trouble behind all of this. I think he set up Jennifer years ago, along with Thomas, to get to Winterfield. I think he was using the construction business in New York as a cover. All that talk about bid-rigging and being pushed out of the business is bull. I think he had one thing in mind from the start: Winterfield's gambling business."

"What do we do when we get there?"

191

"You know son, I think we're walking into a hornet's nest. One thing I do know: Winterfield is not going to jeopardize his whole operation for a family feud. I think that's why he's offered to make peace with Jennifer and Thomas."

The pilot and Winterfield walk out of the terminal. Winterfield joins Joe and me and the pilot heads for the hangar to ready the plane.

"Are you two ready? Are you expecting trouble?"

"Without a doubt."

"I like that. We're going to make a great pair, Mr. Biltmore."

I picture Bogie and Captain Renault walking away from the departing plane in Casablanca.

The pilot has finished his pre-flight check and has started to bring the plane to the docking area. A worker from the hangar wheels the large ladder over for us to enter the plane. Two by two, like the animals in Noah's Ark, we board the plane. First the two gorillas, then Winterfield and Thomas, and finally Joe and I take the stairs to the plane's door. I take a deep breath as I am about to enter the plane. The worker at the bottom of the stairs calls after me.

"Mr. Biltmore, you forgot your bag." He runs over to the terminal where I put it down when I was talking with Joe. I see him place something in the bag and he runs back to me.

He makes his way up the ladder and hands it to me. "Captain Jim says hello."

I'm stunned but I recover quickly enough to look into the opened bag. I see a gun buried within my dirty clothes. I nod my thanks. Boy, the captain gets around.

I board and the door is slammed shut by the co-pilot who must have already been on the plane.

The large radial engines start; we make our way down the ramp into the water, becoming a boat. The pilot hits the throttle and saltwater washes over the windows as we start lifting off the water and into the air. I look at Joe who seems to be handling this better than the last time. I hope he liked this case. I could not have picked a better case to win him over. If it was only a little more exciting! Oh well, it's all I've got to offer. It will have to do.

Chapter Thirty-Two

Another Day In Paradise

The trip over to Winterfield's island paradise takes less than forty minutes. Joe is holding up on this trip, watching the waters below. If we can wrap this up today, I promise I'll take Joe fishing to get his decision on which direction he's going to take in his life. I look at my watch and calculate that Phillip should be here either within the hour or sometime late tomorrow.

The plane that wants to be a boat when it grows up starts making its descent into the water for a splashdown. I hate this part of the flight. The pilot has spotted a wave to hit and, by the feel of the landing, he has hit that one and a few more. The windows are covered with seawater as the floats act like a fat kid, belly-flopping into a three-foot pool. The pilot cuts back on the engines and motors us to the now-familiar dock. My stomach is doing flips thinking about the reception we will get at the dock when Thomas walks out.

Winterfield gets up first, "Thomas, let me get off first. I have a feeling that Jennifer and Martelli will be a bit surprised to see you."

I search the dock to see who might be our welcoming committee.

The pilot opens up the hatch and throws a bowline to a dockhand. The side door is opened and Winterfield struts onto the dock. I figure I better be out there with him. Joe follows me too.

"How do you feel?"

Winterfield looks at me strangely, "This is my island and my business. With one phone call, I can make Jennifer and Martelli disappear for good."

That's the old Winterfield that we've come to love. Mean and nasty. I'm glad he's back. This could get messy. I've grown to like the son-of-a-bitch. In the distance, I hear the sound of the golf carts humming along the path. The sound precedes the actual sight of the cart. I hold my breath. Cart one appears; it's Julie driving by herself. Good. Next, I see cart number two coming through the trees. Driving that is Jennifer. This should be good. Winterfield takes off for the end of the dock. Joe and I follow close behind. The excitement is building. The golf carts arrive at the same time as we do. Jennifer barely waits for the golf cart to stop before jumping out. Julie walks around Jennifer to me and gives me a rub on the back as if to say glad you're back.

"I've been waiting a long time to talk with you," Jennifer says. "My partner and I want a piece of this action or I'll go right to the authorities about your having my husband killed."

Winterfield keeps his cool and looks at me. I can't take this anymore. Jennifer will die when Thomas comes walking out of the plane. From the cabana, Martelli strolls out, holding something behind his back. This looks like trouble. I turn and whisper to Joe, "Go get my bag, quickly."

Joe does not hesitate. There is an awkward silence on the dock. Martelli is walking slowly with his hand behind his back toward us, and I really need Joe to make it back here rather quickly.

Martelli sticks out his hand for a shake. Joe is back and hands me my bag. I quickly open it and turn toward the plane to take out my gun, then turn back toward the action, keeping my gun behind my back. In the distance, I hear a speedboat approaching rather quickly.

Martelli does not wait for Winterfield to shake hands. He pulls a gun from behind his back and points it at Winterfield, pulling the older man toward him.

Julie pulls Jennifer toward her and away from Martelli to stop Jennifer from going with him.

Thomas walks out of the plane.

Jennifer faints.

Martelli is momentarily frozen. "Shit."

The boat appears at the dock, obviously part of Martelli's plan to get Winterfield off the island.

Martelli aims. I push Joe into the water as Martelli pushes Winterfield into the boat and jumps in right behind him.

I aim for Martelli but Thomas comes running from the dock and barrels into me as my shot misses badly. Thomas regroups and tries to dive off the dock after the speeding boat. Julie tries to stop him.

"Let him go," I shout, knowing that the idiot will get about three feet from the dock while the boat is already three hundred feet away. I stare at the disappearing boat and, probably, my big pay-off. College is not looking so bad at this point. I wonder what type of classes I could take. I check out the scene.

Julie makes her way back to Jennifer who is coming from the shock of seeing Thomas. Thomas walks to the beach after his ridiculous attempt to swan dive from the dock after a speeding boat. Joe is standing next to me in disbelief, most likely wondering when classes start.

Jennifer walks angrily over to Thomas who is sitting dejectedly on the beach. Then out of the seaplane comes our answer.

I never noticed the co-pilot who, I surmised, was in the plane in the hangar the whole time. After all the excitement, Captain Jim strolls out.

"Need help, Mr. Biltmore?"

I can only produce a lame laugh and a shrug.

"Would you like to go get them?" Jim offers.

I look at him and then at the plane. I have a sick feeling that he is thinking of some type of stunt we usually see in a James Bond movie. Knowing I cannot fly a plane, it will have to be me doing the stunt.

"What do you have in mind?" I ask Jim, not really wanting to hear the answer.

"Let's find out where they've gone. We have two people who can fly, and you. I'm sure something will come up when we see them. Hopefully, they have docked someplace and I won't have to dangle you from the plane."

Jim walks back into the plane; the radial engines start and I follow.

Joe runs after me, "I'm coming too." I give him a look as if he just hit a home run in the World Series. I can use all the help I can get. I enter the plane with Joe right behind me. We take seats and Jim is about to close the door when Julie walks in.

"I think Jennifer and Thomas have a lot to talk about."

She sits next to me. Jim walks out on the dock, unties the plane, and walks back in, slamming and locking the door. We make a short taxi from the dock, and the captain speeds up the engines for take-off. Through the window I see a speedboat approaching the dock. Phillip has arrived, but we have no time to tell him what's happened or where we're going. I see him dock the boat and Julie points to the plane as we take off. From the window, they seem to be in a very animated conversation.

Jim comes from the flight deck announcing that they can spot a boat in the distance; it seems to be headed southeast – Cuba. From our vantage point Jim says, he doesn't think the boat has any intentions of docking soon, so we'll be able to catch up to them.

"What's the plan, Mr. Biltmore?"

Jim is standing over me. I'm wondering if it's too late to get Forester involved. By the time the Navy got here, they'd be in Cuba or wherever they are headed.

"How slow can we fly without falling into the ocean?" I inquire.

"We can get as low as you want and pretty damn slow, to a point. What did you have in mind, jumping?"

"Do you have a rope ladder on this thing?"

"I'm sure we do. If not, we can use the docking tie ropes. I just don't know if we can go that slowly though."

"Well we can scare them by flying rather low, but I'm sure they'll start firing, and by the size of this plane, I'm sure the gas tanks are rather large and the chances are pretty good we'd end up in South America."

"What about us firing first?" Joe suggests.

"Nice thought son and I'm sure it sounds like a lot of fun, but I wouldn't want to hit Winterfield. I'm thinking of lowering the ropes by the engines to tie up the propellers until I realize this is unrealistic. Hopefully, somebody will stop me. It's a one-shot deal but it beats jumping from this thing. "I think we should make a few low, fast passes at them. Let's see if we can spook them. Winterfield is a pretty smart fellow. He might take action when he seeks help."

We're approaching," Jim says, looking back through the cockpit.

Julie has been silent throughout this plan. I don't think they give this type of training in the FBI.

Joe tugs at my arm, "Dad, what if Winterfield has staged this whole mess with Martelli to get away with all the money?"

The captain pulls up the throttle when Jim taps him on the shoulder. We climb to around two hundred feet and start circling.

Jim comes out of the flight deck. "I never thought about it. This Martelli character is not unlike Winterfield. I don't have any information on him, but it could be. I suggest we buzz by the boat and see what's going on."

Jim goes back to the flight deck and returns with two pairs of binoculars. He hands one to me and he keeps the other. He returns to his co-pilot seat and starts scanning the water. I do the same from the portside window. Julie goes over to a window on the starboard side.

"That was incredible, Joe." I pat him on the arm and gaze out at the boat. What a mind to waste in college.

I see Jim using hand signals to get the pilot to ease off on the throttle and start a slow descend. We're still circling but our circles seem to be getting tighter. The boat is in view. I hold my breath as I put the binoculars slowly into my eyes.

The boat is going full throttle, and Martelli and Winterfield are seated together on the port side. There are no indications that Winterfield is a hostage or that they are working together. I know they see us, but they're just pushing the hell out of the twin Volvo 250s.

Jim calls out from the flight deck, "Look, half a mile due south."

We train our eyes as per his direction. Being on the side of the plane Julie, Joe, and I can see only as we circle. Finally, we see it, a cruising yacht the size of an aircraft carrier, or so it seems.

Jim rushes back to us, "It has to be two hundred hundred feet." The pilot calls Jim back, "Jim take a look at this thing."

Jim heads back with binoculars straight ahead. The pilot has stopped the circling and is headed for the yacht. I cram myself into the flight deck with Jim, as Julie and Joe try to look over my shoulders.

The custom-fitted yacht has lowered its stern wall into the ocean. The speedboat is headed right for it. It's a damn loading ramp. The speedboat slows down as Martelli pulls a wire at the engine wall and releases both his motors into the water. The speedboat runs up the ramp with sparks flying everywhere but, since the engines are now floating in the ocean, there's no explosion. Since our eyes are focused on the speedboat we don't see a deckhand holding a machine gun on the aft deck. The pilot, thank goodness, does and pulls the stick toward him and the right as hard as possible, causing the plane to swerve right and up, throwing all of us back into the cabin.

We seem to be out of range when Jim comes back to check on the sprawled bodies.

"We're going back. They have an Apache helicopter on board, and since we do not fly as fast, it's better if we head back." We all agree.

"I guess you were right Joe; very good."

"What's our next move, Jamaica? Do I have to call you that?" Julie asks.

I bend over and whisper, "My name is Winston."

Julie looks at me with a crooked smile. "Jamaica it will be."

We straighten up and head back toward the dock. I pull my cell phone from my pocket and dial Forester to bring him up to speed. I feel the plane about to land in the waters by the casino. "Hi, it's me." I quickly filled him in on the immediate activities. I made sure the rest of the group could hear when I gave the location. "Right now, we're about seventy miles northeast of Cuba. That's right, Cuba. I don't think that's where they're headed, I'm thinking South America. It's not much fun spending millions of dollars in Cuba. Any ideas?" I listen for a while before ringing off.

"What's up, Dad?"

I have a small audience. Julie and Jim heard my end of the conversation, but want to hear what Forester had to say.

"It seems there was a small revolt in the Cayman Islands. The Minister of Finance has been implicated with Senator Johnson in a money scheme starring our Mr. Winterfield. Johnson started naming names and places. Some very powerful people in Washington invested some money with Winterfield, and he was going to start another

202

gambling operation on another private island by the Caymans. Once Johnson started talking, the United States put pressure on the Caymans to freeze Winterfield's assets. That's when this minister got panicky and ratted out Winterfield, who was going to scam all the investors and keep the money for himself. Their little plan blew up, and now the Navy will be waiting for Winterfield when he gets there."

"That's great, Dad."

The plane lands without any of us knowing. I like that. Phillip, Jennifer, and Thomas are waiting on the dock. Jim throws the line and Phillip ties us up. We disembark and stand in the scorching heat on the dock.

CHAPTER THIRTY-THREE

A HUNCH

"Can we go inside? I can use a beer."

Jennifer walks head down toward the cabana right off the beach. We all follow. The air conditioning of the cabana rejuvenates me. Phillip walks to the bar and starts the refreshment order. Thomas and Jennifer have reunited it seems, but they are stepbrother and sister, even though not related, but the thought gives me the willies.

Jennifer walks up to me. "Mr. Biltmore, I'm truly sorry. Thomas explained his end of the story. He was out to protect himself; that's why he staged his own death. Somebody was out to get him and he thought it was Winterfield, or at least his associates, not knowing all the time it was Martelli. Martelli set us all up."

"I think our work here is done," Phillip chimes in.

"Thank you, Tonto." I finish my beer and turn to Jim, "How about a ride back?"

"Whenever you're ready, I'll be on the plane."

Jim walks out. My cell phone rings. It's Forester. He informs me that the Navy has picked up Martelli and Winterfield. He has orders to ship them to Washington.

"Thanks. Joe and I will see you before we head home. I don't know; you'll have to ask him when you see him." I close the phone.

"Winterfield and Martelli have been captured and are heading to Washington. I would not stay here too long," I tell Jennifer and Thomas. "The United States Government will probably confiscate this place as evidence." I don't care where they are headed. I still feel something is up. "By the way, I think I still need to get paid."

Jennifer nods in agreement. She retrieves a suitcase from the corner and carries it into the bedroom in the corner of the cabana. She walks out a minute later and hands me a small overnight case. I don't open it, but thank her and head out the door. Joe and Julie follow right behind. Something is bothering me.

We walk the long dock to the plane. We all get on and Jim prepares for take-off. I open the cell phone and call Forester. "Something is bothering me. I just don't trust Thomas and Jennifer. They're on Winterfield's island. Okay."

I turn to all, "He's going to send someone down to pick them up."

The ride back to Chalks Terminal is silent. I'm tired, both physically and mentally. I need to close my eyes and run through this story. I take one last look at our band of travelers. Julie and Joe are fast asleep; Phillip is jotting down some thoughts, probably for a new book.

My mind races: Why did Winterfield need Martelli? Winterfield had the world by the balls. He could have gotten rid of both Thomas and Martelli when they were just small-time construction owners. How did Martelli know that Jennifer would fall for him? Why did Thomas kill himself in the first place?

Let's start there. Thomas knew about the gambling stuff and used the construction business as a front to try to get this operation from Winterfield. He probably grew up listening to all his exploits and pieced it together. Martelli comes along with a plan to help Thomas get to Winterfield. Where did Martelli come from? I'm thinking he was Gino's eyes and ears. Neither one knows Gino is dead. Okay, Gino needs someone to watch over his end; that's Martelli. Winterfield does not like partners, but he's probably scared of Gino and not of the other partners. Guys from Washington and Vegas don't scare him. Makes sense. Now if Jennifer does not fall for Martelli, this thing blows up for Martelli, who's trying to get his piece of the pie. After Thomas's death, Martelli thinks it's time to get out of Dodge before Winterfield kills him too.

I open my eyes. Phillip is writing furiously. "What's up?"

Phillip looks at me and I at him; we both figure it out at the same time: "Jennifer."

She set this whole thing up. She and Thomas. She knew Thomas was not dead, but they both needed to find Martelli. Martelli was the only one who could rat them out to save himself. When I met them on the island they were both keeping up their parts of the scam, not knowing the other one was just waiting for Thomas and Winterfield to show up. They both used me to bring them here. Martelli had his plan and Jennifer had hers. She had a better plan.

I quickly call Forester. "Get a cruiser to that island and stop them from leaving now." I hang up. "Jim, do we have enough fuel to go back to the island?"

"No. We need to get back to the terminal. What's up?"

Everyone is awakened by the sound of my conversation with Jim. The cell phone rings again. "Get out of here. Okay, fine. I'll see you within a couple of hours. Thanks, buddy."

"The Navy has picked up Thomas and Jennifer. In the cabana, they had three suitcases full of cash. The officer in charge figures it's around a couple of million dollars."

"That doesn't seem like a lot of money from the amounts we've heard about, Dad."

"You're right, Joe. Navy intelligence picked up a computer transfer from that island to an off-shore account in Thomas' name for the amount of four hundred million dollars."

Again, with all the chatting, we land and don't even notice. I'm starting to get the hang of this seaplane stuff. We taxi up the ramp and finally walk out of the plane, and down the stairs with another case solved.

Jim walks over. "It's been fun. If you ever need my help, please call."

"Thanks for everything." Phillip walks over and shakes Jim's hand, "I'll send you a check for your troubles." Jim pats him on the back, "Write about me kindly in the next book. I need to be younger though." Phillip laughs. "I'll get a cab."

Phillip and Jim walk into the terminal. Julie and I have an awkward moment. Joe senses it and follows Phillip.

"What's your plan, Miss FBI?"

"I don't know. This was fun. I have to be back at work in the morning. I'm sure I'll have to testify in Washington about this case."

"Don't bet on it. I've learned over the years that when politicians are involved, these cases sometimes go away."

"What's Joe going to do?"

"I don't know."

"Call me when you get settled. How is New York?"

"Within a month or two it gets cold. No fishing."

"It's always nice down here."

I can't take this anymore. I kiss Julie and promise to call. She slowly walks away.

CHAPTER THIRTY-FOUR

CHANGE IN DIRECTION

It's been three months since the case closed. The papers never mentioned a word about it. Forester retired right after sending his prisoners to Washington. No one heard anything about them again. Winter is setting in here. I look around the bar; Phillip, Bobby, and I are the only ones here. Phillip's halfway through his book, so it keeps him very busy. Oh, about that overnight bag: it contained one-hundred-and-fifty thousand dollars, not bad. The ringing phone echoes throughout the bar. I pick it up. Caruso walks in for his morning coffee.

He seems to have brought with him five people who just happen to arrive for breakfast at the same time.

"Hello? Hey, Joe, how's school? Are you doing okay in the dorm? What?" I'm having trouble hearing him. I walk toward the window, away from the crowd. "What happened? No, really. Okay. Put him on." I listen intently as the President of the college explains that one of the professors, a young woman and the head of the football booster club, has vanished with all the funds they received from The BleepYou.com Bowl that the college has just played in. They can use all the help they can get without word getting out. Would I be interested in coming down?

I survey the bar. It's not the same since Joe left. I don't blame him. The case showed him it was very important to make his mark in the world. We decided that going to college in Florida is a good thing since Uncle Bill could keep an eye on him. I took him to the plane and watched him leave. He wanted to go by himself and I promised I'd let him be until spring break when I would come down and we'd go fishing for a week. It broke my heart to see him go, but I knew I had to let go.

"Let me speak with Joe." The president puts Joe on the phone.

"Do you think this is a good idea for me to come down now?" I hold my breath and listen.

"It was? I hope you didn't build me up too big? Okay, I'll catch a flight in the morning. I'll see you at the airport. What? I don't know. Let me think, okay? See you tomorrow. I'll call in the morning with the flight information. Bye."

Phillip looks over his coffee, "Well, what was that all about?"

"That was the president of Joe's college. Two people have vanished with all the money from TheBleepYou.com Bowl three days ago. Joe told him about me, and they want me to come down and see if I can find the money without making a big deal about it."

Caruso looks at me. "The timing seems right. I put my papers in today. I have enough days off built up where I can actually get out now and still get paid full salary for three months before my pension kicks in. How about some help?"

I look surprised. "Sounds great. What about you Phillip?"

"I guess I can always add a few chapters to the book if this case is anything like the other one. I'll go too."

I have a thought, an impulsive one, but a thought. I look at Bobby. He's such a good kid. I dig into my pocket and pull out the keys for the bar. I throw them to him.

"All I ask is that you do not sell this place without talking to me. A deal?"

Bobby is stunned, "It's really mine?"

"It's all yours. Keep in touch. Let me clean out my stuff in the back."

I walk into the back office and throw whatever things I want to take into a duffle bag: two nickel-plated 9mm guns, some cash from the safe, and a signed Reggie Jackson baseball from my desk. It's time to change locations. I've been working out of this same place for longer than I can remember. This last case has put me on the map, but more importantly, I want to be where my son is. My band of merry travelers can relocate wherever the case leads us. Phillip has no real family unless you count Joe and me. Caruso and his wife always loved to travel, and his kids are spread out all over the map. He's put his time in, and now he needs a break. I hope he's not going to be a stick-in-the-mud about the gun issue in Florida.

I look around this place and the memories, good and bad, wash over me like a tidal wave. This was Joe's home. He did his homework here, had friends to play here and, most of all felt safe here. Now he's gone and I need to be near him, at least for my well-being. I'll let go when I can. He called me, right? I'm not the one calling him for help, but since he did call, it's the least I can do.

I'll call my lawyer and have everything transferred to Bobby's name. I will not look back. I made the best of a bad situation and now life moves on. I need to go where life takes me. I guess the situation is right too. It's easy to say as long as the cards fall into place like now.

I close the door behind me, throw the keys to Bobby, and head into the next chapter.

CHAPTER THIRTY-FIVE

THE GANG'S ALL HERE

I'm the first one off the plane. I see Joe at the other end of the security gate. I walk through quickly, giving him a big hug. He looks good. I don't notice Julie and Jim standing behind him, and they don't notice Caruso and Phillip walking toward us through the crowd.

We're all here. "I have a four-by-four ready for us, Dad."

Joe and I walk in front of my band of merry men... and women.

"Something worries me, Joe. This is an awful lot of mouths to feed for one small missing person's case. How much did they vanish with?"

Joe whispers in my ear, "Five million. I got the president to agree to expenses and five percent of what we recover."

"That's my boy, or should I say 'partner'?"

Made in the USA
Middletown, DE
12 March 2022